CONFESSIONS OF AN ILLEGAL ALIEN

CONFESSIONS OF AN ILLEGAL ALIEN

by
Irma Noriega

Copyright © 2000 by Noriega, Irma

All rights reserved.
No part of this book may be reproduced, stored in a retrieval system, or transmitted by any means, electronic, mechanical, photocopying, recording, or otherwise, without written permission from the author.

ISBN: 1-58820-159-7

This book is printed on acid free paper.

1stBooks – rev. 10/28/00

To my son and daughter,
> You have gladdened and given utmost meaning to my life.
> I will forever love you.

CONFESSIONS OF AN ILLEGAL ALIEN

BACKGROUND

It was difficult to maintain the equanimity that Alexandra needed when her thoughts were far away and she felt so dissatisfied with what she was doing. Compelled by circumstances, she still could not ascertain why things developed in her life this way. Just a few weeks ago, she still had been unemployed and without money, walking the streets of Salt Lake City, filing applications here and there that had been stacked in piles on someone's desk, until finally she had been hired in this clinic.

"Something is better than nothing," Alexandra had repeated to herself after a year of trying.

The inequality and injustice she had always opposed here were always present in the faces of the homeless who came to the clinic to get help, and in the asperity and insensibility with which her coworkers treated them. Alexandra felt trapped underground. The oppressive feeling in her chest reminded her that getting this kind of job could not be all her expectations in life.

Every minute she spent at the clinic seemed an eternity, as if she were climbing an immense escalator where each step took her further away from her dreams. Making a living consumed all her energy and time, and this fact filled her with deep dissatisfaction and discomfort.

Alexandra Marquez walked about the clinic's reception area and looked at Marsha. Marsha was sitting at the front desk, her mouse-like eyes behind her glasses were staring at Alexandra with disgust. Marsha was a scrawny, self-conceited newlywed who walked with a stiff neck and treated everyone in the clinic as if they were inferior. She had a straight and long nose and a tiny mouth that she curved to the left with despotism.

How many more patient's charts is Marsha planning to hide this time? Alexandra thought.

Marsha had been her enemy since she had started to work in the clinic, trying to undermine Alexandra's work, making her appear as a fool when she couldn't find the charts that Marsha had purposely hidden or misfiled alphabetically with the sole purpose to demonstrate how foolish and inept Alexandra was.

Alexandra was tired of that job. It didn't provide her with a third of what she used to earn when she worked with Enterprises 2000 to make a decent living.

She went to the window. The mountains were covered with snow and blurred by the grayish sky anticipating the coming storm. Alexandra was in her late thirties, thin and slender. Her brown eyes had a nostalgic and daring look. She was quiet and reserved with strangers, but when she was with friends, she knew when to be serious, funny, and seductive. She was wearing a purple dress that delineated even more her splendid figure. Her long and wavy hair fell loose to her waist in dark golden curls that resembled corn silk.

"I need some staples--do we have any?" Alexandra asked.

Marsha opened the nearby drawer fastidiously and handed her a box of staples.

"Have you figured out how to reload the stapler?" said Marsha with a malicious and sarcastic smile.

Alexandra blinked. It wasn't worth answering. It was a sickening game, only for a sick mind like Marsha's. Marsha was one of those people whose only purpose in life was to make others miserable.

Alexandra closed her eyes. Two people were behind the desk requiring her attention. She walked towards them as she asked courteously, "may I have your name please?"

But Marsha, knowing the patients, pushed her aside.

2

Yesterday had come and gone quickly, taking away her childhood dreams that had been buried with her mother's corpse and the brutality of a drunken father. Alexandra closed her eyes, saddened. The screams of the fight grew louder and closer in her mind like a volcanic eruption, causing her legs to tremble.

Her father walked in abruptly, pushed the bedroom door open with his feet, and in rage lifted her up, then pushed her to the floor.

"Come clean the floor, you little idiot," he said, beating her repeatedly with his feet as she lay on the floor where she had fallen.

She began to cry copiously, helpless and scared.

"Shut up, you fool!" Alexandra's father slapped her face with his big hand, giving her a bloody nose. "I am going to hit you real hard this time, so you can cry for a good reason." His eyes were firing with rage.

She got up and followed him silently to the living room. Tears were still falling from her eyes as he continued to push her. Alexandra's mother was sitting in the corner near the window, sewing and crying desperately. Mariana, her oldest sister, also crying, had started to clean the floor. Alexandra glanced at her mother and the sewing machine in fright. Her mother was always there behind the sewing machine, day and night, tailoring precious and fine clothes that she sold to feed them. Then she glanced around. Cans of beer and empty bottles of wine scattered on the floor gave a sour and revolting smell to the room. The pot of beans, two gallons of milk, and broken glass were also spread across the kitchen floor. Her father pushed her again and Alexandra fell on the mess near her sister.

"Clean." he uttered sternly, "until I can see my reflection on the floor like a mirror."

In the near bedroom her three brothers, awakened by the noise, cried loudly. Her two little baby sisters were perhaps still asleep.

"Let him die, God, let him die," were Alexandra's nightly prayers.

He gave them life to make them suffer. Alexandra hated him and her mother's passive attitude that submitted her to his abuse, his insolence, and his irresponsibility. Inflicting pain on them was like a game to her father, who would break into laughter seeing their anguish. He had lost his job, and since then had started drinking saying he did not fit in a world of idiots. He was in his thirties, tall and strong. His wavy black hair, green, luminous and alert eyes made a perfect contrast with the whiteness of his skin. Her brothers and sisters feared him; his proximity meant only one thing--punishment and torture. He had varied and ingenious ways to inflict punishment. The sound of his steps produced shivers up her spine and a cold sweat on her hands. Alexandra glanced at her sister Mariana as she worked on the floor with her in silence.

The immense collection of books in the fine baroque bookcases seemed to stand out in sardonic contrast near the mess. Balzac, Kant, Shakespeare, Sartre, Dostoevski, Nietzsche, Dante, Tolstoy, and the Greek classics were silent witnesses of Alexandra's misery and phantasmagoric friends who came to life for her. Her father knew the contents of those books one by one. He delighted in reciting them and rejoiced in his family's ignorance when he made the whole family gather around the table to listen to his verbosity. Hour after hour, he laughed and called them fools as he pounded his fists on the table and slapped their faces again and again, teaching them the lessons of the wise.

3

Her mother's death stayed in her mind, paralyzing her in pain. So many years had passed since then, but the memories still danced in crude agony, leaving her immobile and without strength. She sat down and her childhood years became once more present....

Broken glasses, loud clamors, and cries came suddenly from the living room. Alexandra wrapped her young head in the covers, almost fearing to breath. She would have liked to disappear and disintegrate to stop the sound of her father's outrage. Who was being beaten this time? Her brothers? her little sisters?

For a moment, everything was silent, she didn't know. In the dark she could imagine butterflies that had a myriad of colors like brilliant stars and rainbows, covering a world of beauty.

Alexandra's mother opened the door and came into the bedroom. "I don't feel well," she said in a hollow voice. "I am very cold."

Alexandra stood up, startled, and looked at her mother in the dark. The intense fear that she felt so many times when her father hit her covered her body as she started to shiver.

"Mom, what's wrong?" Alexandra asked, about to cry, frightened to hear the answer.

Her mother's body was quivering, like a leaf pushed by a strong wind. Her teeth were chattering.

Alexandra's sister, Mariana held her mother's hand and took her to her bed.

"Lay down here, mommy, on my bed" Mariana said as she pulled the blankets to cover her mother's body, which kept shaking harder and harder under the covers.

"I have a horrible headache," their mother said as she began to moan.

Alexandra and her sister couldn't talk; they stood paralyzed, praying hard.

"Dad might have hit her," Mariana whispered to Alexandra as they sat at the edge of the bed, perplexed in the face of the unknown.

"We need to take her to the hospital," Alexandra said after a while. Their mother's skin was cold and her eyes had grown immense, submerged in dark shadows as a prelude to death.

They got dressed and went into their father's bedroom; he lay drunk on his bed, snoring. They closed the door quietly and looked at each other in grief. Even though they were thirteen and fourteen years old, they knew that their mother's life was in their hands. The nearest hospital was thirty blocks away, but it didn't matter. For them, no fear was greater than seeing their mother sick. They opened the front door and stumbled into the lonely and dark Mexico City night. The bells of a nearby church echoed the time in the darkness--three o'clock in the morning.

Two days later, Alexandra's mother died. Her mother turned immobile and rigid as the last breath of air escaped from her chest to return to her Creator....

4

After her mother's death, it seemed like everything in Alexandra's mind had turned to silence; the whole world stood suspended in a blank and dull sensation. Without her mother, the house had been left lifeless, illuminated only by a lugubrious mantle. From every corner of the house, voices and familiar sounds seemed to emerge, bringing back bizarre, disconsolate, and kaleidoscopic pictures. Behind the sewing machine the ghost of death sat still watching.

There was no one around. Her little brothers and sisters had disappeared to hide their loneliness and abandonment. After the burial, a lot of people dressed in black came to the house to say prayers in a strange, lethargic and melancholic chant called "the Rosario" to ensure the salvation of the recent dead.

"Why did you leave me, Mary?"

In the middle of the night, the scream sounded like it came from beyond or from hell. Alexandra wrapped herself in the covers. Outside her bedroom, her father paced from one side of the house to the other crying in pain and in delirium for his wife. "Why, Mary? Why? Why did you leave me?"

Doors opened and closed in the empty and gigantic rooms that would never hear again the echo of her mother's voice...Alexandra felt so full of terror. Her brothers had started to cry as their father's steps approached the bedroom door. Death had extended its cold hands towards them, leaving them at their father's mercy.

Death was a mystery. Alexandra was scared of it. In her mind the image of the four doctors attempting in vain to revive her mother's heart was always present. Even now after many years had passed, it was hard to reconcile what followed. In the blink of an eye, her brothers and sisters had been dispersed by adults who disposed of their lives as they wanted. Her two little sisters were taken to an orphanage while the family argued amongst themselves to determine who would take care of who, and her eight, nine, and ten-year-old brothers ran away. Only Alexandra and her oldest sister stayed in the house with their father, building barricades at night, behind their bedroom door, to prevent their father from getting in to beat them.

5

"Some Mormon missionaries are coming to my house this evening. Would you like to come?" Rosa, Alexandra's eighth grade classmate asked her loudly as they copied the assignment from the blackboard.

"Some what?"

"Some Mormon missionaries," replied Rosa. "They are from the United States. Would you like to come?"

"You have to be kidding!" Alexandra rebuked.

"No, I'm not!" Rosa exclaimed. "I am serious."

"Be quiet back there!" the teacher yelled from the front of the classroom.

"What time are they coming?" Alexandra whispered.

"5:30 p.m.," Rosa replied.

"I'm not sure if I can make it, but I'll try."

"Quiet, I said, or I'm going to have to separate you!" the teacher threatened. Alexandra and Rosa smiled and quieted down.

If she had not accepted Rosa's invitation to go to her house that evening, Alexandra reflected, she would never have met the Mormon missionaries. But pulled by uncontrollable curiosity, she went.

When Alexandra arrived at Rosa's house with her sister and Hilda, a childhood friend, Rosa and her family were already gathered in the family room with Bibles in their hands, forming a semi-circle around the missionaries.

"Hurry," Rosa said, "we are about to begin."

In silence they also took a place and waited with increased curiosity for what the missionaries had to say. Alexandra could still remember the missionaries' smiling and bright faces.

Looking back at the events of that evening, Alexandra remembered a scripture she once read: "To everything there is a season, and a time to every purpose under Heaven: a time to get, and a time to lose; a time to keep, and a time to cast away.." Undoubtedly, that day had been the right time for them. God, in His ever present mercy had seen the precarious situation in which they were left after their mother's death, and He had, like a caring father, come to their rescue, to offer them through these missionaries the gift of Christ.

Reading The Book of Mormon had been more than just reading. It had opened her heart and offered a new glance at possibilities. It was another Testament of the divinity and ministry of Jesus Christ. As she listened to the Mormon missionaries' message that evening, something in her heart had clicked. For her, it had been like climbing to a mountaintop and looking at a verdant valley for the first time.

As for her sister Mariana and Hilda, they too had been deeply touched by the missionaries' message.

"It was not possible to hear their forceful words testifying about the atonement of Jesus Christ, the eternal nature of the family, the purpose of life, and remain unmoved," Hilda expressed.

It was strange for Alexandra to think how the meaning of things varied when they were viewed from different perspectives. The missionaries' words had all of a sudden changed her despair to hope, and her insecurity to certainty.

At home, even though her father had raised his family under the rigorous indoctrination of the Catholic Church, he was an atheist. He hated all religious groups.

"There is no God," he would say. "I am God. I am the only God." And, believing himself omnipotent, he would criticize anyone who did not measure up to his sophisticated parlance and wisdom. Her father also hated Indians, gringos, and blacks.

"Milk and oil don't mix," he repeated again and again.

It was a creed her father took pride in. His beliefs clashed with Alexandra's and Mariana's beliefs, who, subjected to his ordeals many times, had learned to dislike and disregard anything their father liked.

That day had been a very special one, besides the good tidings of the Gospel, they had met two very handsome boys: Warren Maxwell and Gavin James--two missionaries of the Church of Jesus Christ of Latter Day Saints. They both were very handsome and nice, but Warren, Warren had like stars in his limpid blue eyes, Alexandra noticed it as he shook her hand.

"Missionary work is the way that the Church Saints, better known as the Mormon Church, spread its message around the world," the tallest missionary said, "we leave our homes for two years to testify that Jesus is the Christ. We don't get pay, we are glad to do it because we want others to know the joy of the restoration of the Gospel."

It was a precedent message. Something that instigated them to such an extent that when the meeting was over, they couldn't wait to meet with them again to hear about their church a little more.

Going to church became the Sunday affair. To attend, they escaped their house through the roof jumping to the neighbor's house and exiting across their yard unto the street. The Mormon Church was twenty minutes walk away from their house. It was exciting to be there hearing the message of peace, learning that if they followed the teachings of Jesus they would find happiness, live righteously, and a proven way to ameliorate all the stresses of this life.

Once the services were over, they visited for a while with friends to engage in heated debates about what they had just learned. Braulio, Nina, and Sally among others, were always there. They had been members of the church for a few years. They knew well the principles of the church, and they were truly devoted to their beliefs.

"Self-mastery, can't be determined by how much knowledge one person has acquired, but by that person's ability to be sensitive, even in the worst of circumstances, towards his or her fellowmen. Don't you guys agree?" Braulio said.

"I agree." Nina said.

The discussions were always a blast and being with friends gave Alexandra a real sense of joy. Then, in church, there was also Warren holding her hand for more than one minute when he said "hello" as he looked deeply into her eyes.

No matter what retribution awaited them at home, the time at church was well spent.

6

Then it happened. One morning, during her freshman year at the University of Mexico, she met Jules. She had gone to the main library to study for a test, and there she was introduced to Jules by Carlos, one of her classmates.

Jules was black. As Alexandra looked at his skin, charcoal against the sunlight, she pondered for a moment all she had heard about black people--all she had heard was hate!

He was the first black person she had personally met and she was quite curious. Perhaps this was the opportunity that she needed to challenge and to disprove her father's beliefs.

"We have a party on Saturday night," Carlos said as he handed Jules a piece of paper with the address where the party was going to be held. "We'll be glad to have you there man."

Alexandra's heart stopped. The thought of seeing Jules at the party produced in her a sudden and strange excitement.

Alexandra banished her thoughts for a moment and paced nervously about the clinic. It was so easy to recall the past. It seemed like a movie rolling in front of her eyes. She sat near the window, looking out into the distance. The sky was totally gray and the snow outside fell on the ground like a laced mantle. She took a deep breath. A long time had passed since her little brothers ran away and her little sisters were taken to a boarding home. A long time had passed since the day when they were all finally reunited and sheltered by their grandmother, while their father was left to live alone in the house where he had been so cruel to all of them. A long time had passed since the day their father came to their grandmother's house to live with them again, transformed and unrecognizable, a prisoner of his own soul.

"Open the door!" Alexandra's father had yelled as he knocked at the door frenziedly.

He was skinny and disheveled, as if the alcohol and pain had consumed his defiant poise and stature of old, only to leave a grotesque caricature of what he once had been. He looked humble and apologetic, a shadow of despair and loneliness in his eyes.

"I love my children, Esperanzita. I want to live with them. I can't be alone anymore. I beg you, let me in!" he pleaded crying. "Forgive me!"

Alexandra looked at her father through the glass door and felt a deep pity, and for some reason unknown to her, she felt the need to run and hide to avoid looking at him, the giant who had transformed into a dwarf.

"You killed my daughter with your vice! You mistreated her constantly. You are a brute and an indecent man!" Esperanzita screamed hitting him on the chest with her bony fists.

Since they came to live with their grandmother, they had only seen him from a distance, drinking with the neighborhood drunkards and vagabonds on the street corners. Once in a while, they had seen him lying in the street where he had fallen, like human garbage, consumed by alcohol.

7

Jules came to the party with some friends, and soon asked her for a dance. He was an expert dancer, and Alexandra felt as if she were floating off the ground, wrapped in the strange and unknown pressure of his arms.

Jules was from Haiti. He had been a student at the University of Mexico for the last two years pursuing a Ph.D. in Sociology. He resided in the U.S. and he would be graduating at the end of the current year.

"I feel," Jules said, looking directly into Alexandra's eyes, "that this won't be the last time I am going to see you. God makes things happen--for you and I this is a special occasion, I know. It is a time that will bring us together for always. You'll see."

Alexandra looked at him attentively. "Why are you saying that?" she asked shyly.

"Because when I saw you, I knew you were the one I want to have forever in my life," he replied.

"How old are you?"

"Twenty nine," he said with a smile, "and you?"

"Seventeen," she said.

My father is wrong, Alexandra thought. The blacks she had met tonight were friendly, intelligent, educated, and respectful. They talked of Europe, Haiti, politics, music, books, and love, with such warm and captivating voices that she could have listened until the daylight.

Jules was tall and courteous, his movements poised and elegant. His cheeks and mouth were smooth and well defined, and when he talked, his dark eyes glossed sometimes with sadness, and at other times, they seemed to smile playfully like the rays of the sun upon the sand. Alexandra couldn't lie to herself, Jules held a great attraction for her. His presence and his laugh aroused in her sentiments that until now she never knew she had.

8

The lights were dim and resembling a misty twilight when he kissed her.

"I will come back to marry you, or I will send for you," Jules said passionately, pushing her away a little to look deeply into her eyes. "I have to go back to New Orleans. My permit has expired. My sister is looking forward to meeting you." He continued cautiously, sensing her tense feelings, "time goes by quickly. It will be a matter of just a few months. You'll see."

Alexandra believed him. Since she met Jules only six months had passed, but she loved him dearly. Everything seemed unreal, diffused, and distant except for his touch of fire at this moment. She embraced him innocently, melting warmly in his arms.

"Show me that you love me," he whispered as he continued to kiss her this time softly. Alexandra looked at Jules incredulously and pushed him firmly.

"We can wait," Alexandra said, hurt. "If you love me and you are going to marry me, we can wait."

Jules was too smart to keep trying. "I am sorry," he said and left, leaving behind his promises to come back in the near future to marry her, and her empty heart.

9

Was it lot or coincidence that Thomas came into her life? It was hard to tell, but it was Jules who introduced him to her on graduation night. Thomas attended evening classes in the medical school. His school was on the opposite side of Campus, yet somehow he managed to be outside Alexandra's classroom every night to walk with her to the bus stop.

The single door that served as entrance and exit to the classroom, left no alternative for her but to confront him. Every night at 10:00 p.m., ever since he met her, there he was, leaning against the classroom door with the books and newspaper under his left arm, smiling with that constant, almost permanent smile that widened his eyes. Alexandra didn't know why, but that smile irritated her.

Thomas was tenacious. He did not take no for an answer. Despite the fact that she had tried to dissuade him many times not to be outside her classroom, her denials seemed to inflame his innermost desires even more, because he had come on to her with even more persistence than before.

"Hi," she greeted him reluctantly.

"Hi," Thomas answered. He followed her with precise steps throughout the school corridors and then towards the gate that led to the Campus walkways.

From Alexandra's school to the bus stop was a fifteen minutes walk, and crossing the Campus at that hour of the night was dangerous.

"I love you, Alexandra, I love you," Thomas told her fervently that night as they were walking towards the bus stop, suddenly holding her tightly. "I can't resist what I feel for you any longer. You must know this by now--you are such a pretty and attractive girl."

The campus field was deserted and dark, and Alexandra was scared, fearful of Thomas' passion. She glanced around nervously. Many men were like Thomas, she had heard. Love for them differed nothing from sex, and they tried the impossible to get it.

"I love Jules," said Alexandra, pushing Thomas away. "We are going to get married at the end of this year and you know it."

"No, I don't know it," Thomas answered fiercely, forcing his kisses on her and breathing heavily.

He was a sexy man. He always dressed impeccably.

"I love you, more than Jules does, can't you see it?" he continued. "I wouldn't have left you behind as he did."

Thomas seemed to have lost control. He took her hand firmly and he brought her close to his body, squeezing her against him tightly.

"I want you," he muttered. His voice sounded deep and suffocated; his dark eyes were gleaming with lust. They were standing near the east side of the administration building, and abruptly with one sole movement he shoved her against the wall and kissed her again and again, trying to force her. Since the first time he had seen her, he had had visions of wrapping her in his arms, fusing her with his very soul.

"Thomas, let me go," Alexandra begged. "Please, let me go."

Thomas released her unexpectedly, wiping away the sweat that had appeared on his face. He had gone too far, but possessing her for a moment was all there was in his mind.

"I'm sorry," he said, trying to disguise the urge that compelled him. "I don't know what came over me. It is hard to control this feeling when I see you. You are like an obsession to me."

Alexandra grabbed her books and ran away into the dark, shaking and crying.

Thomas stayed behind. He wanted to run after her, but instead he stood still, his arms hanging limply and helpless.

10

All of what Alexandra knew about sex she had learned in 9th grade, watching a movie while her classmates whispered things in each other's ears accompanied by short and malicious laughs. Alexandra's mother, raised in the old fashioned way, had never told them anything about sex. When Alexandra had her period for the first time, Alexandra thought she was dying.

"Something it's wrong with me," she told, Mariana, " I have a lot of blood in my panties. Maybe, I'm going to die."

"You are not going to die," her sister replied, "Mom told me that once you are eleven years old, all women bleed for a few days each month."

"Oh." Alexandra exclaimed. "Did she say anything else?"

"Only that. There are some paper towels in the bathroom. Use them if you need them." Mariana said.

The explanation didn't make it feel better. She walked into the bathroom feeling awkward. Talking about sex at home was forbidden.

Watching the movie at school still did not make much sense.

"Why are you guys laughing?" Alexandra asked confused.

"Don't be a fool!" said one of her classroom friends. "Men put their things inside the women's body so they can have babies, then the women carry the babies in their stomach until the babies are born."

Alexandra blushed. She didn't want to hear anymore. She wanted to cry. At home she had been told that storks brought babies and she had believed it. Mom had lie. She did not trust them with the facts of life to teach them. To know the truth second-hand was like a gruesome joke that increased her insecurity.

"If I ever get married and have children, I won't abuse them, or lie to them," Alexandra said to herself, not understanding why her mom hadn't been straightforward with them.

11

She stopped washing dishes at the sound of the doorbell. It was Warren. She hadn't seen him for the last six months, ever since he was transferred to Acapulco to service there.

"I'm going back home. My time as a missionary is over. I came to say goodbye." Warren said smiling reaching for her hand.

He hadn't changed, if anything, his skin was tan.

"Time goes by so quickly--I am going to miss you Warren." Alexandra said.

"If you are going to miss me," he said, "why don't you go back with me. My mother will adore you."

She looked at him, disconcerted, not fully understanding what he was saying.

"How could I go back with you Warren?" she exclaimed playfully. "I live here, in Mexico--are you kidding?"

"No. I'm not kidding. You can marry me, and go with me to the United States."

Only then she got it. Warren's words were as serious as the Church teachings that said it is not possible to get to the celestial kingdom without getting married for all eternity in the Temple.

"Warren," Alexandra said timidly, "I can't marry you--not now, anyway. While you were in Acapulco on your mission, I met a guy at the University, and I am going to marry him," she confessed, thinking of Jules.

Warren blushed.

"Alexandra, are you sure you don't want to marry me?"

"I'm sure!" she replied. "I am in love with Jules."

She accompanied him to his car, where his missionary companion waited. She held him tightly and said goodbye.

Warren got inside the car, pulled the window down and shouted. "You know where I live if you need me."

Alexandra waving her hand smiled.

12

After her father came to live at her grandma's house, his appearance in a matter of weeks deteriorated rapidly. He looked pitiful, decrepit, and skinny. His skin had purplish tones. He wouldn't eat and paced around the house like a living shadow, crying and reciting poetry, or he sat on the ground in the backyard talking to himself and to their mother, as if she were still alive.

Alexandra did not hate him anymore. It was a thousand times more preferable for her to see him as he was before: a tyrannic inflexible sadist, than to see him in this deplorable pseudo-human condition where he had lost all sense of dignity.

One day, unexpectedly, her father left to seek his fortune. He left with the vagabond and drunks of the neighborhood to another city, clinging to his last, desperate attempt to survive. Alexandra looked at him with real pain and walked away from him. The few clothes they had and their schoolbooks wouldn't disappear anymore, stolen by their father to sell them for a few pesos to buy liquor.

Remembering that day, Alexandra imagined how much he must have carried on his back when he left. Besides carrying the load of loneliness and the deep sense of failure. None of his children told him goodbye or wished him good venture. They all blamed him for their misfortune, their mother's death, and their poverty.

Their grandmother didn't have a steady job; she supported them by doing some sewing and by borrowing some money in the neighborhood out of the pity they inspired.

In Mexico City, getting a job wasn't easy. No one wanted to hire minors, and without a job recommendation from someone of importance and renown, the chances of getting hired were remote. Mexico City was immense. It took Alexandra two hours by bus to get to the University, and two more to come back, but the trip was worth it. She loved going to school. From the classroom windows as far as her eyes could see, the valley extended to the South in all its beauty. In the South East, the Popocatepetl and Ixtlaxihuatl, the highest mountains peaks, crowned the scene like two inseparable lovers kissing each other behind the clouds.

It was beyond compare to learn while her eyes filled with the splendor of creation as the sun set in the West, leaving behind a touch of pink and gold over the grass and clouds. The moments spent in school were for her always exciting, adventurous and fun. She loved to hear the echoes and voices of wonder, laughter, joy, and hope in the students and teachers.

13

Inexplicably, Jules stopped writing. His words of love and promise ceased, and Alexandra felt distressed and confused. She was doing laundry pondering about Jules' silence. when the bell rang. Nina was at the door. Since they met at the Mormon Church, they had become inseparable.

"I have a surprise for you," Nina said, walking in with her characteristic poise and conciliatory gesture. "I know the reason why Jules stopped sending you letters."

"You what?" Alexandra exclaimed, looking at her friend in surprise.

Nina, had a slight smile on her face. She was slender and possessed a rare beauty. It was not only because of her physical attributes, but because perhaps her beauty radiated from within delineating every one of her features. She had a heart condition, and when she talked she ran out of breath easily. Nina had met Jules at one of the weekly school dances, and from then on, they had become the best of friends.

"He sent me a letter explaining why," said Nina, full of satisfaction. "He said," Nina paused, breathing hard, "that Thomas told him he made love to you. Jules believed him, he says he can no longer marry or write to the one who betrayed him with one his friends while he was gone." Nina paused to catch some air. "The letter also says, that he has been lying in a hospital bed for the last six months being treated for tuberculosis. Here is the letter; see for yourself," Nina sat down as she handed the letter to Alexandra, looking at her with genuine concern.

Alexandra took the letter, shaking, not believing yet what she had just heard, and began to read.

"Oh, that Thomas!" Nina was saying. "It is amazing what he has said and done to get your love." Her voice turned harsh and low.

Alexandra's eyes were wide, reflecting the great disbelief and deep pain that she felt.

"I'll write to Jules and I explain that Thomas is lying," Nina said with conviction. "Jules can't be such a fool as to believe such a thing of you."

"Don't!" Alexandra screamed, hurt. "Please don't. I'm not sure what I am going to do yet, but I'll think of something."

"As you wish," Nina said, walking towards the door. "I have to go home now, my mother is waiting for me. I'll see you in the chapel on Sunday."

"Thanks," Alexandra said, giving her back Jules's letter. "Thanks for taking the trouble to come all the way here to let me know about this. I appreciate it."

Nina just smiled.

After Nina left, Alexandra wondered how a thing like this could have happened to Jules. First he had hidden his illness from her. Now, with Thomas' intrigues she knew Jules had one more weight on his spirits.

14

Contrary to what she expected, when she came out of class the next evening, she found herself face to face with Thomas. She glanced at him quickly; he was well dressed. The cashmere and leather jackets that he always wore matched perfectly with the dark color of his skin. It was perhaps the intensity of his smile that caused the brilliance of his eyes, Alexandra didn't know, but it irritated her. The flow of students walking out of the classroom pushed her closer to him, but this time she ignored him, speeding down the corridor among the crowd.

"'Alexandra, wait," Thomas called.

Alexandra turned to him abruptly. "Why did you tell Jules that we made love?" she fired at him.

"In love and in war, there are no rules, Alexandra. Everything is possible," he answered without a trace of shame.

"In love, and in war?" Alexandra repeated, puzzled. "I never thought of love as a war or as something you have to fight for in order to get it..." Her voice faded. She seemed to be reflecting on her last statement.

"In love and in war, whoever comes out with the best strategy wins, didn't you know that?" Thomas reiterated emphatically.

"Whatever. It was very low of you to have done such a thing." She looked at him angrily as she went rapidly down the stairs. Specially, when Jules is so sick in the hospital."

"Jules is in the hospital?" Thomas asked, surprised, "I didn't know he was sick."

Alexandra looked at him with resentment as they continued to walk across the Campus.

"I did it because I love you--don't you understand?" He said exasperated, pulling her with force towards him. "He is there, I am here! I can make things right for you," his voice, over her mouth, was low and impetuous.

"No, you can't! In fact, you made all things wrong for me with your lies. I don't love you. I love Jules. You are not going to see me anymore. I have decided to go to the United States to see Jules. Once I am there, he will ask me to marry him. I am quitting school."

Thomas drew her closer feverishly. "You are making a mistake."

"Let me go," Alexandra demanded, looking coldly into his eyes." I want to remember you as a gentleman. Let me go!"

She escaped easily from his arms. At no time had Thomas thought that things would end like this.

15

A week later, Nina died. At her return from school on Monday evening, Nina's mother and Alexandra's sister were waiting for her with the news.

"I hope I am not intruding," Nina's mother muttered, alarmed and desolated, standing up when Alexandra came into the room. "My Nina had a heart attack this morning, she is in the hospital, I came...." she broke into convulsive sobs. "You can go to the hospital to see her."

Nina's mother was in her sixties, but she looked older now. She had dark hair, dark eyes, and fleshy lips. Her face was swollen and wrinkled with pain, and her whole body quivered. Nina, besides being the support of her house, was the only reason that her parents' troubled marriage had kept going. Nina's terminal illness and her kindness had kept them together.

"I'm terribly sorry," Alexandra said, feeling an incredible sorrow as she held Nina's mother by the arm. "Let's go."

"Grandma, grandma!" Mariana cried out. "We are going to the hospital with Nina's mother to see Nina. We'll be back in a couple of hours."

"O.K." Their grandma replied from the back room.

In the hospital, in the ICU unit, inside a respirator, Nina was fighting for her life. Through the small plastic window of the respirator, Alexandra and Mariana slid their fingers to touch their friend's hands. Nina could no longer talk, but she stared into their eyes while Alexandra's and Mariana cried. Nina squeezed their hands to say goodbye. The next day, Nina was buried facing east, in the manner of the Mormon creed waiting for the resurrection of the dead when Jesus would come again. They left the cemetery in silence. Once more death had come to remind them how ephemeral and unpredictable was existence. Laughter, dreams, movement, love and continuity at the side of her dead friend were fading. Alexandra and her sister, attracted by a sound, raised their eyes to the sky. A flock of birds was peacefully crossing the sky at that moment. They looked at them in awe. The soul of their friend was perhaps at this time flying like those birds to another sphere that, according to their religious beliefs, was invisible yet real.

Their small world of friends little by little was disintegrating. Braulio and Sally had married and moved to Canada, Warren had gone back to the United States, and Nina, had died.

THE TRIP

In 1967, the United States of America stood in the minds of all people as a land of wealth, and for that common vision, the United States was precisely the place she soon would be going. Her sister Mariana, and Hilda, had departed to the U.S. a month ago. They had gathered the earnings from their temporary jobs, and without giving any thought other than to start a new life and make money, they had flown to San Francisco. The latest news Alexandra had from them was that they were working and that as soon as they would send her airplane ticket, Mexico would be history. She smiled.

Hilda hadn't had a clear motive to go other than not wanting to lose the friendship of her two best friends. She was the only daughter of a well-to-do family. Her parents had always been very complacent with her, conforming without hesitation to every one of her wants. It was for this reason, that she had been intrigued by the possibility of an adventure that would dissipate the boredom of her predictable and stable life.

As for herself and Mariana, there were simply too many reasons to leave. In Mexico there was no tomorrow. Their childhood dreams had been buried by catastrophe and disintegrated by sorrow long before their mother had died due the irrational impositions and punishments that their father had inflicted upon them. So for them, striving and facing the pangs of the unknown seemed the most plausible way to come to terms with themselves and put the past to rest. Mexico offered no choices to overcome their financial limitations. In the United States, there was no doubt in their minds they would make money to help their brothers and little sisters, and find the happiness that until now had escaped them.

Dropping out from the University, was the toughest decision that she had to take. She loved learning. But the last months of class, had been very hard, especially when she had no food in her stomach or money to pay for the bus fare to go back home. Studying under those conditions, and digging daily for every penny to make up the thirty cent bus fare to take her across the city to attend school, was more than exhausting. It was then, that Alexandra had the clear understanding of how poverty keeps people immobilized due to a lack of stamina, energy, and resources, and also how this lack of energy and resources could easily be misinterpreted as irresponsibility and laziness in the poor.

17

"If you are going to the U.S., don't go to San Francisco," Monte said. "New York is the place to go. There are tremendous opportunities in New York. I can refer you to my best friend," he added, assuming a sophisticated pose while puffing slowly on his pipe.

Monte was the best friend she had at the University. They had met at the medical school, attending one of her mandatory classes. He was thin and refined, a cavalier. Looking at and listening to him was a delight. His voice was hoarse and quiet, his gestures precise, his suit immaculate, the smell of his fragrance delicious. The expensive scarf that he always wore around his neck, gave him a special and manly touch. He was French. He had been in many parts of the world, and it was impossible not to notice his polished and cultured manner.

"Listen, take this note with you, and there will be no problem. I will let him know that your sister and Hilda are going too. Franz is like a brother to me. He'll help you." He took a piece of paper and as he spoke, he wrote some lines on it, and handed it to her.

"I don't know how to thank you," Alexandra said.

"No problem, anytime, that's what friends are for." He stood up and came close to her, drawing on his pipe. "Take care of yourself, and send me a note when you get there."

"I will." She stood up and held him.

He smiled kissing twice on her cheek. She kissed him back, then, she left.

18

To get a passport and visa at the United States embassy took three hours. She rode the bus home dazed, like in a dream. This is it, she thought. She packed a few clothes, said goodbye to her grandma, her brothers and little sisters, and departed to the airport. She had thirty dollars in her pants pocket, and a one-way ticket to New York.

The voice coming through the intercom interrupted her thinking. "Delta International announces the departure of flight number 18. Passengers going to New Orleans, please board the plane by Gate C."

Her heart began to pound. New Orleans! It would be just a matter of hours before she would see Jules after more than a year since he left. The end of their relationship had been so unfair. She couldn't wait to see him and to tell him that Thomas lied.

She held her little suitcase and walked across the hall among the crowd of people. Airports were an interesting place to be. This seemed to have a peculiar glamour, a distinct sound, like a buzz of euphoria. People moved in all directions rapidly, lined behind the ticket counters with a sense of importance, or waited with anxiety by the gates.

She was so excited to go, now more than ever. She boarded the plane, sat, and the plane took off. After a while, she looked through the window. The clouds were underneath now, white and brilliant like immense cotton balls in the limpid sky.

19

New Orleans was a city of mystique, cadence and warmth, with an exuberant climate and vegetation, and the permanent aroma of rain and plants. Alexandra didn't remember ever before seeing so many black people together. She walked resolutely towards the airport customs. There, an immigration officer stamped the visa in her passport and welcomed her to the U.S. She told him she was on vacation, thanked the officer gracefully and went to get her luggage.

Outside the airport the sound of the crickets was as intense as the heat. By the main entrance, half a dozen taxi limousines parked. Without vacillation Alexandra took one.

"Bridge City, please."

The taxi driver looked at her with curiosity. He was big, fat, and dark. His immense eyes resembled two bright lanterns shining in the night.

"That's a black town," he said. "Are you sure that's where you want to go?"

Her heart began to pound wildly.

"This is the address," she answered, handing him a piece of paper. "Is it far away?"

"No," he said, glancing at the paper, then at her. "Fifteen minutes across the river." He took the luggage from her hands and opened the limousine's, door to let her in. He closed the door behind her as he began to hum.

The surface of the Mississippi River reflected the street lamps like small, flickering diamonds. Two ships were sailing slowly across its channel, perhaps bringing goods ashore. The view was majestic.

"Here we are," said the taxi driver as he turned to the right. "This is Bridge City. We just need to find the address."

Black children playing on the dirt road stared at the limousine, surprised, and started to run behind it. A line of unpainted, small, and run-down houses were on both sides of what seemed to be the main avenue. Three bars were on the intersection where several black men and women were laughing, drinking, dancing, or simply standing by the porch.

"It's a white! It's a white!" The children clamored, pointing at her with suspicion when the limousine stopped.

"Hush! Go away!" the taxi driver said as he came out of the car to grab her luggage and open the door for her.

The children scattered in several directions, then stopped at a short distance away.

Alexandra paid the taxi fare, and the taxi driver left. From the distant bars, soul music could be heard faintly. She looked around for a minute as if she were lost, and then at the house in front of her. She was frightened. The children and some adults who had come out of their homes were standing near, looking at her. She knocked at the door shyly. An old, black, toothless woman opened the door, surprised.

"Is Jules home?" Alexandra asked. "I am a friend of his from Mexico. I just got into town."

The woman walked right back into the house, leaving the front door opened. Two or three minutes later, Jules was at the door looking at her shyly.

"Come in," he said, carrying her luggage in. "What are you doing here?"

"I came to see you," Alexandra murmured, following him.

Inside the house, everything was clean and modest. The old toothless woman was sitting in the living room with two fat women, watching television. As they crossed the room, the women looked at them, whispered something between them, then, broke out in loud laughter.

"She is a friend," Jules addressed them politely and kept walking towards his bedroom. He was obviously nervous as he turned to Alexandra. "I am going to take you to my sister's. She lives around the corner. You can't stay here."

Jules's bedroom was almost in darkness, illuminated only by a dim light that he had at one side of the dresser. Everything in it was in order and cleaned as if the room had been recently dusted. Nothing was fancy. He had a small yellow radio, an alarm clock, a spacious and smooth bed, some books lined up over a dresser, and a painting of Jesus at the head of the bed. The photograph that he and Alexandra had taken before he had departed from Mexico was over his bureau. The room was hot and humid, and her heart was aching and trembling.

"Let's go," he said, taking her by the hand as he got his wallet.

"O.K" she answered.

As they walked on the street the children started to follow them, pointing at her and howling, "We don't want whites around here! We don't want whites around here!"

"Don't worry," Jules stated, seeing her apprehension. "I know them all. It'll be all right. Hush!" he said, turning to the kids angrily.

Down the street, Jules's sister was glad to meet her. However, Jules' sister looked as embarrassed as Jules had been when he first saw her standing by his door.

"I am pleased to meet you, child," she said. "Jules said a lot of good things about you."

"Did he?" she asked.

Jules' sister was married. Her house was smaller and much older and deteriorated than the house Jules lived in. It consisted of two rooms divided by a small curtain. There was one double bed by the entrance, a sewing machine in the corner, and a small television over a stool. In the kitchen were a shabby table, a stove, a sink, two chairs and a telephone on the wall. There was no bathroom.

"We'll sleep on the kitchen floor so you can sleep on the bed," Jules's sister offered. "It is very hot around here, and we have lots of roaches. Big roaches, child. I hope you feel comfortable."

Alexandra felt a great tenderness towards them. Everything was different than what she had expected. She had not imagined she would see this poverty, not in the U.S. As for Jules, he didn't say any more, only "Good night." Then, he left.

"We have no bathroom," Bella explained apologetically as Willie, her husband, smiled nervously, rubbing his hands. "We have a basin. There it is, if you need to use it," Bella pointed at the corner. "I am sorry."

"Please don't worry. I am already taking your bed...I am fine, thank you," Alexandra said cheerfully. "Good night."

"Good night, child."

A little sheet divided the two rooms. She got under the covers and tried to sleep. Through the walls she could still hear the buzz of the crickets that seemed to increase in pitch as the night went by.

The lonely sound of a train approaching woke her up. She didn't know what time it was, but she looked out though the window. The moon was shining with splendor in the sky. The noise of the train approaching grew closer, and as it did, the ground seemed to rumble to its very core. A distant cock began to crow, followed by silence.

20

When Alexandra got up, Bella was cooking breakfast. Her husband had left early to work, and on the small table hot pancakes and milk were neatly arranged.

"Good morning, child, come and sit down," she said with a smile. Her skinny figure contrasted grandly with her big stomach. She was pregnant and due any time now.

"I brought a little something for you, Bella," Alexandra said as she extracted out of her suitcase a small box. They had just finished breakfast.

"Why did you do that?" Bella said, touched with emotion. She unwrapped the present rapidly. "Oh, child, thank you. It's beautiful!" She smiled happily, modeling the silky nightgown. "This is just what I needed."

"I am glad you like it. I wasn't sure what to buy, but when Jules talked about you, and he mentioned that you were married."

"I will wear it for Willie tonight," she said, winking.

"Oh, you are?" Alexandra smiled as she walked towards the door. "I want to go downtown. How far is the bus-stop?"

"You can catch the bus that goes to New Orleans on the corner," Bella said pointing towards the east side of the street. "It will take you straight to the heart of town. I would go with you, child, but I have a doctor's appointment in about an hour."

"Don't worry," Alexandra replied, "I understand. I can go by myself. It'll be all right. I'll be back in a few hours." Alexandra kissed Bella, got her purse, opened the door and walked out.

"Don't forget to call me if you get lost," Bella said.

"I won't. Thank you. Bye now."

"Bye, child."

Outside the sky was tranquil and blue. Some black people on the street passed her and said hello. There were no whites in the area. She got on the bus, paid the fare, and sat in the rear, looking absently through the window.

"Miss." The bus driver stopped the bus abruptly. "You cannot sit in the back," he yelled angrily. "It's for blacks."

"Oh," Alexandra said, blushing as she moved to the front of the bus, disconcerted and embarrassed, not yet knowing exactly what was going on.

The bus driver gave her a dirty look as she moved to the front, and he resumed driving, convinced that he had accomplished his duty. The four black men riding the bus with her didn't move, but continued to look down pensively. A knife-like pain took hold of Alexandra's heart. She had heard of things like this, but it was shocking to have to experience them.

In the daylight the small black village disappearing behind seemed smaller and poorer. She looked with perplexed eyes at the driver. He was a middle-aged man, with blond hair and blue eyes. The monotonous sound of the engine seemed to blend with the buzz of the mosquitos and beetles flying in all directions over the flowerbeds. It was the late sixties, the time of the Beatles. How is it still possible that this kind of discrimination exists? She wondered.

Alexandra breathed deeply. Racial differences were less turbulent in New Orleans than any other city, Bella had explained. However, it was very hard for Alexandra to understand how people here or anywhere could be framed and separated that way for reason of their color, when virtue and human value were raceless and colorless.

The Spanish French architecture of the Vieux Carre was a delight. Two and three story cottages with balconies and patios dating from colonial times gave the area a picturesque and special touch. Art galleries, boutiques, sidewalk cafes, night- clubs, twining plants and layers and layers of flowers mingled all together.

The St. Louis Cathedral in the midst of the plaza stood majestically as a vivid honor to the Creator. She walked, fascinated, admiring the surroundings. A flock of doves soared to the sky as she approach them, chirping and agitating their silvery wings that shone in the sun.

She went around the fountain and put her hand in the water, then, stood still, listening to the warm notes of Dixieland that seemed to saturate the air in a city where blacks and whites blended in paradoxical contrast.

"Child," Bella told her when she got back, "I have asked the woman who owns the store to let you take a bath in her house. She is the most wealthy woman in this neighborhood, and the only one who has a bathroom." Her tone was quiet.

"Thank you," Alexandra answered. "Don't worry about me. I will be leaving tomorrow."

Jules' sister's bathroom was outside. It was a little wooden room with a hole on the ground without a toilet or shower that was shared by several neighbors.

"Let's go anyway," Bella insisted. "I know you are not used to these things."

Bella was right. In Mexico, before Alexandra's father started drinking, they had been affluent. Then they were poor. Sometimes they had only bread to eat in the whole day, but they had always had hot running water, a place to take a shower, and a toilet.

21

Mrs. Jackson, the store's owner, had a big house and the biggest red lips Alexandra had ever seen. She was corpulent, around fifty years old, and well groomed. She wore heavy make up, and when she opened the door, she was chewing gum.

"Come in," she said proudly, with a big smile. "The bathroom is right here. Please follow me."

Alexandra followed her in silence. Mrs. Jackson was very solicitous and affable. It was obvious how proud she was of the position she had in the community and how unusual it was for her to be asked to allow "a white" to take a bath at her house.

"Thanks," Alexandra said, a little inhibited before the awkward situation. "I don't know how to thank you."

"Don't mention it," Mrs. Jackson said, opening a nearby closet. "Here you'll find the towels, shampoo, body lotion, and soap. Help yourself." She walked towards the door with an air of superiority, bouncing her hips and her arms on which she wore heavy and enormous bracelets.

Inside the closet, half a dozen towels and other toiletries were neatly arranged. Alexandra got a set, got undressed and jumped into the shower. The cold water cleared her head and let her muscles rest.

22

That evening around eight o'clock, Jules came. He still behaved shyly and didn't look directly into her eyes. He stood at one corner of his sister's room and kept looking down as though avoiding her. He was no longer sick. He had eventually recuperated from his illness, and the doctors had released him from the hospital after eight months.

"I can take you around if you want me to," he said. "We can go to a cinema, and have something to eat if you like."

Alexandra smiled tenderly and walked towards him, taking his hand. "Of course I want to," she said. "Let's go."

Jules took her to a movie. The theater was located in a black neighborhood in New Orleans. The ticket window read: "for blacks only".

Jules parked the car across the street from the theater and asked her to wait. "Just one minute," he said, "I'm going to see if they will let you in."

Jules ran across the street, and the next minute he was back. "It's fine," he said. "Let's go."

The film was good, but in such an unusual environment, Alexandra didn't feel comfortable. She was in the midst of a world she had never imagined, where people were segregated and separated from others for the sole reason they were black.

The cinema was ugly. A very small and dim room in which she could only hear the audience's presence by the effusive applauses and screams that came every so often as the movie went on. During the show Jules held her hand tightly in an unspoken gesture of reconciliation. It wasn't much, but for her Jules' silent gesture meant more than hundreds of words he could have said.

After the show, Jules took her to a motel located in the black neighborhood, and there, without kisses or words of loving, he made love to her. Then, he drove her back to his sister's home.

The trip was made in silence, each wrapped in their thoughts as they sat in the car without looking at each other.

"Blood is a sign of purity." He stated, while he held her forcefully in the dark. The physical pain she was feeling shut off the disappointment of her soul. Without saying a word, she got up and took a shower. Her body ached.

In the early morning hour, the singing of the birds already announced a new day and a new beginning. Alexandra got out of Jules' car and walked silently inside his sister's house. She packed her things quietly, avoiding thoughts about what had just happened. Three hours later, after Jules came again to pick her up, they were at the airport. New York was now her next port.

At the airport, Jules seemed distant. He didn't look at her much, nor talked. Nevertheless, she had been his, and for Alexandra that was all that mattered. Despite the disappointment she had felt in his arms, she was now convinced that an indestructible lace had tangled their lives forever.

Faster than she would have wanted, the goodbye came. Jules's sister held her tightly, and Jules extended his hand to her in a mute gesture of farewell. She rushed through the gate, turning her head again and again until she could no longer see them. After a while, comfortably seated in the airplane cabin, the thick clouds seen through the airplane window resembled a beautiful golden platform where her soul, compelled by the beauty, went running to kiss the sunrays. She looked ahead with a smile. Life was exciting and beautiful.

The applause of the passengers interrupted her thoughts when the plane touched the ground safely. Alexandra got her little suitcase and followed the crowd that moved frantically from aisle to aisle. She pressed Monte's letter tightly in her hand, left the airport and caught a taxi. The taxi cab sped up rapidly, leaving Kennedy Airport behind.

23

From the east side of the Brooklyn Bridge, driving along the freeway, the view of the city was overpowering and superb. The immense skyscrapers seemed to blend with the blue sky, and to the left, the Statue of Liberty emerged from the water, extending her hand of welcome as a reminder of freedom, opportunity, and the inextinguishable fire of human hope.

A black dwarf with big black eyes and an attractive smile opened the door and looked at her with surprise.

"I am looking for Monsieur Boudreaux," she said. "I came from Mexico. Monte and I are friends. I met him at the University of Mexico.."

"I am he," the dwarf said, putting his hand on her shoulder inviting her to come in while his free hand reached out for her luggage.

"Sit down," he said as he himself took a seat.

He seemed so pleasant and affable that Alexandra's momentary fears were dispelled, and she felt at ease and at home.

"Thank you," she said, handing him the letter that Monte had sent him. "This letter is for you."

He read attentively for a moment as he rested one hand on his chin. His features were soft and nice, and his smile open and frank. He could have been tall and handsome, if it hadn't been for the enormous hunch that deformed his body.

Suddenly, he paused. "Monte, mentions that you have a sister and a friend. Where are they?"

"At the moment they are in San Francisco, but they will join me as soon as I call them to let them know that I made it up here."

"Come," the dwarf said, standing up and walking down the hall. "I'll show you where your bedroom will be from now on."

Alexandra stood up and followed him as he held her by the hand.

"I don't know if you know," the dwarf explained, "but Monte is like a brother to me. You'll like it here. New York is an exciting place. You'll see."

He opened a door to the left and walked in.

"You and your sister and friend will sleep here." He put her suitcase inside the closet. "Please, make yourself at home." He walked out of the room. "By the way," he said coming back in, "I live with a cousin. She takes care of the house. She is not here right now. Tomorrow, I will take you to get your social security card. You will need it to get a job."

"Thank you," Alexandra replied hesitantly. "I am a little nervous about going there."

"Don't worry about it," he assured he. "The only thing they'll ask you for is your passport--you have it, don't you?"

"Yes I do," she answered.

Well," he said, "I promise you, tomorrow they will issue your social security number right away. You'll see." With that, he walked out of the room, smiling and closing the door behind him.

When he left, Alexandra sat at the edge of the bed and looked around. The room was spacious and clean; it had a queen size bed in the middle with a navy blue quilt, a bureau with a white phone and a silver clock, a dresser on the right with an arrangement of gardenias, a gorgeous lamp, and an intriguing painting on the wall. She closed her eyes. Her recent experiences had been so varied that her head seemed to whirl. She hadn't had time to analyze them in detail, but at first glance, she realized how deceiving appearances could be. She recalled her recent visit to New Orleans, the impressions she received there, and now, her meeting with Mr. Boudreaux. There was no doubt he was a dwarf, but a giant in his heart. Just a few minutes had passed, when she heard some knocks at her door.

"Alexandra, can I come in?" asked Mr. Boudreaux.

"Come in," she said as she got up, passing one hand over her hair.

"This is my cousin Mimi," said Mr. Boudreaux happily, opening the door and smiling pleasantly. "This is Alexandra," he explained, addressing Mimi, who did not seem very excited at

Alexandra's presence. "Monte sent her. They are the best of friends. She, her sister, and a friend will be staying with us for a while."

Mimi mumbled some words in "Patois," the Haitian-French dialect best known as "Creole," and looked at Alexandra coldly. She was wearing a dress of vivid colors, and her hair was hidden beneath a tight flowery scarf. She was brown, short and fat. She had a big round head, and big black circles around her eyes, so black and different from the brown tone of her skin color that they resembled a half mask. She mumbled something else to Mr. Boudreaux, then, she turned around.

"Don't worry, she is all right," Mr. Boudreaux said apologetically. "She doesn't speak English well, but she likes you."

Alexandra had a feeling that she didn't, but right now she was too tired to think. She half smiled as Mr. Boudreaux walked out of the room leaving her alone once more. After that, she fell asleep.

24

The Social Security office swarmed. The noisy crowd lined up in two endless lines; one in which to submit the documentation and another where people waited their turn to pay and to receive a social security card. Alexandra was trembling, but her fears had been unfounded. There was no problem. By the time she got out of the building, as Mr. Boudreaux had promised her, she had the social security card. Mr. Boudreaux smiled at her with true joy.

"You see, I told you that it was simple. The only thing you need now is to get a job." He held her hand amicably, put his hat on, and walked with her to the subway. "I'll show you where I work, and then I will show you your way around downtown."

"O.K," Alexandra said.

Down in the subway tunnels everything was old, humid, and dark. The sound of the approaching train produced a deafening roar and such a tremor and violent draft that the train boarding station seemed to be tearing apart. As soon as the train stopped, a human river came rushing out while another rushed to get in.

"Hurry," Mr. Boudreaux shouted. "Let's get in."

Alexandra jumped in nervously. Inside the train most of the people read newspapers, and others, with empty eyes, seemed to look at no-where, lethargic perhaps by the sound and vibration of the train.

Mr. Boudreaux worked in a major firm in New York. He was in charge of the computer department. The building was enormous, luxurious and elegant. Heavy cushioned carpets covered the floor, extravagant paintings hung from the walls, and a variety of adornments and flowers decorated the offices. The porter who stood at the entrance, as well as everyone else who Mr. Boudreaux encountered as he entered the building, saluted him affectionately, a greeting that was immediately reciprocated gleefully by Mr. Boudreaux as he lifted his hat and bounced the cane that he carried with him everywhere he went.

It was noticeable that he was well loved and liked by all. Despite his condition, he had no complaints. The world for him was simply a happy and dazzling place.

"Alexandra," Mr. Boudreaux said, "there's some employment agencies in town, walk around and you'll see them. The streets are numbered. You can't get lost. I will meet you here again around one o'clock to have some lunch. You'll have no problems."

"I won't, don't worry. Thank you very much for everything. I will see you here at 1 p.m." She kissed his cheek twice and went downstairs.

Outside, she couldn't help but look up. The height of the buildings hardly allowed the sun's rays to get through. She was in New York, and it was good. She felt extremely happy, like soaring to the very sky that now she could barely see.

As she walked down the street, she had a feeling of power inside and her enthusiasm increased. Nothing that she could try or do at this moment would be impossible. Not now that I have come this far, she thought. Her thoughts went suddenly to Jules. For a moment her heart trembled. Shaken by doubt, but recuperating as fast as she floundered, she was again secure with the assurance that everything would be fine, and that soon he would ask her to marry him. She just had to wait.

At the employment agency the interviewer, a blond woman with a bright smile, had just told her that she had passed the aptitude test.

"When can you start?" the blond woman asked.

Alexandra couldn't believe it. Before responding, she breathed deeply trying to catch some air to sound natural.

"Anytime," she said.

"Tomorrow?" The woman inquired.

"Sure," Alexandra answered enthusiastically. "Thanks."

"Good," the woman added, handing her some papers. "This is the schedule you'll be working. This is the address, and this is the name of the supervisor you'll be reporting to when you get there. Tell him I sent you. This is my card. Good luck."

"Thanks," Alexandra responded kindly. With the instructions in her hand, she thanked the blond woman again, said goodbye, and left the office.

Down the street she caught the subway. She got off on Times Square and walked two blocks east on Forty Second St.

The hotel where she was going to work was immense and pompous. It was located on the corner of Madison Avenue and Forty Second Street--one of the most frequented zones in New York. Its superb lobby connected to Grand Central Station. There, people swarmed from everywhere. She was amazed. To get that job hadn't been troublesome at all. Everyone she had spoken to had thought she was Jewish, born in New York, and she hadn't denied it. She couldn't wait to give the news to Mr. Boudreaux.

The next evening her sister Mariana and Hilda arrived in New York. And two weeks later, they too were hired to work in a hotel. Monte was right, Alexandra thought, New York is the best place to be if anyone wants to work in the United States.

25

The sound of the music in the Haitian nightclub where Mr. Boudreaux took them that night had a sweet and sensual tone. It was under a dim, reddish light, and the couples dancing in the crowded place moved and sang rhythmically to the sonorous tune.

Monsieur Boudreaux was exhilarating. His immense eyes had an unusual spark. With a smile he introduced them to all his Haitian friends who had approached him solicitously to greet him as soon he walked in.

"Whiskey for everybody," Mr. Boudreaux said loudly leaving his cane at one side of the table that had been reserved for him "At once. Mr. Boudreaux." Said the waiter.

The Haitian club was located on Broadway Boulevard. Broadway divided the Island of Manhattan in half and separated west and east Sides. The club was an elegant place. It was decorated in red tones. Fine tablecloths cover the tables, and beautiful candles served as centerpieces. The band was in the corner. Alexandra felt a little dizzy with the music and the contagious fervor that seemed to come from everywhere. She closed her eyes momentarily; Jules came in her mind. He was wrapping her waistline with his arms and kissing her with that warmth that turned her a little crazy.

"L'amour ce la vie! ne ce pas?" The Haitian dancing with her asked holding her a little tighter towards his body.

She smiled graciously and pushed him back softly, trying not to be rude. Then she talked and talked of everything that came to her mind to divert him from his tenacious conquest. Despite the ineffectual efforts of her new acquaintance, it was a great evening. She loved to dance and to let her sensitivity show with the rhythmic movements of joy. In the semi-darkness she looked for her sister and friend. They also seemed to be having a good time. They were dancing like everyone else with wild joy at the invigorating rhythm of the music and the dancers' chants that seemed to increase in frenzy as the time went by.

All Haitian parties were that way, Alexandra heard someone say--euphoric moments in which to share romance, passion, and fun.

26

Three weeks later Monsieur Boudreaux knocked at their door early in the morning. He had such a circumspect and grave look that it foretold trouble.

"You have to move," he began slowly, leaning on the dresser. "My cousin Mimi is uncomfortable having you here. I am sorry I have to do this to you, but I don't have any other alternative."

"We understand," Alexandra said with regret, trying to hide her fear as she gazed at Mariana and Hilda rapidly. "You have helped us more than enough. It's hard to have three additional people to support."

"It is not that," he said with sorrow, "it is Mimi. I thought she liked you, but she doesn't. You know how strange she is."

During the four weeks that they had spent at his home, Mimi's hostility towards them had grown. Everyday as soon as they came in the house, she went inside her room, slamming the door with disgust and murmuring in Creole.

Mimi was very possessive of the affection of Monsieur Boudreaux, and it was easy to recognize that she had grown very jealous of Monsieur Boudreaux's sympathetic attention towards them and had asked him to have them out of there.

"I know it is hard for you girls to move out on such short notice," Franz continued, "so I have arranged with an uncle who lives in Brooklyn to let you stay with him until you can get a place of your own." He seemed very sad and distressed about the situation. "I wouldn't have asked you to leave, but Mimi has always taken care of me," he explained, constrained. "She is like a mother to me, and I can't oppose what she has asked me to do. You understand my position, don't you?" He stood up and patted them sorrowfully on their shoulders.

"Franz, stop it," Alexandra said. "We understand; thank you for talking to your uncle. We appreciate his help. We don't have any other place to go."

"When do you want us to move?" Mariana interrupted, opening the closet and taking out the suitcases.

"I'll take you there this evening when I come back from work. My uncle is expecting you girls." He looked at his watch. "Well," he added, "it's late, I have to go now. I'll see you guys later." He then rushed out.

After he left, Mariana, Hilda, and Alexandra looked at each other with desperation and began packing their few belongings in silence. The short four weeks of their stay had made them realize how unsafe and lonely New York could be. Opportunity, money, and ostentation were everywhere, but so were diffidence, poverty, and filth.

"The dead and those who are lodged freely take three days to stink," Hilda said, "This is exactly what has happened to us here. We have stayed here longer than three days. What are we going to do now?" Her eyes were wide with dread and anxiety.

"Nothing," Mariana said. "We just have to wait and see."

Alexandra merely nodded as she continued to pack.

27

Mr. Boudreaux's uncle lived on Parkway Ave in Brooklyn. He was married and had a teenage daughter. He was around forty years old and was somewhat attractive. His dark eyes had that kind of melancholic gleam that she had always seen glistening in black people behind their immense eyelashes. At this moment, he was talking to Mr. Boudreaux in his dialect. Alexandra, Hilda, and Mariana couldn't understand what they were saying, but it wasn't hard to imagine that it was about them.

"You can stay here for a few days," Mr. Boudreaux addressed them with his habitual politeness. "They don't have an extra bedroom where you can stay, but you can sleep in the living room in the meantime."

"Yes, thank you," Mariana said.

Standing by the master-bedroom door was a woman they assumed to be Mr. Boudreaux's uncle's wife. She was around thirty-five years of age and was staring at them with discontent and misgiving. Like most Haitian women Alexandra met, she was wearing decollete clothes girded sensually to her body and a bright scarf that covered part of her long, black, well-ironed hair. She was tall, good looking, and robust. She had large red polished nails and her unfriendly eyes, after examining them in detail, were now paying close attention to her husband, who, while he spoke with Mr. Boudreaux, was unable to hide the great attraction that he felt for Hilda.

Alexandra, Mariana, and Hilda could barely remain calm. The whole situation was awkward, but unfortunately, there was nothing they could do. The few racial encounters that they had had during their short stay in the U.S. had proven to them that there were double standards. The antipathy was not only from whites to blacks, but from blacks to whites. Both sides appeared and acted as if they felt misplaced and threatened by the presence of the other. Finally, after half an hour of intensifying tension, Franz Boudreaux stopped chatting, left, and they went to bed, wishing and praying for a better fortune.

28

The man in the car looked at them with curiosity. They were standing on the corner. They had three suitcases with them and they looked scared. The truth is that they had no one to turn to, and nowhere to go. He drove around the corner slowly, and after some hesitation, he got out of the car and walked towards them. This was the heart of Brooklyn, and evidently, judging by the way they looked, they couldn't live nearby. No whites walked that neighborhood.

It was one o'clock in the morning. An almost terrifying feeling began to come over Hilda, Mariana, and Alexandra, when they saw the man.

"What can we do now?" Hilda said, frightened, as she began to cry.

"I don't know," Alexandra answered.

That evening Alexandra had gone to work as usual, and when she returned, at half past midnight, her sister and friend were standing in the corner waiting for her with the news.

The man drew closer. "Is there something wrong?" he asked, stuttering.

"Well," Mariana said calmly, "the woman with whom we were staying threw us out. She didn't like to find her husband talking to her when she came home." Mariana pointed at Hilda.

The man gazed at them quietly. He was in his thirties. He was wearing second hand clothes, had his hands in his pockets, and as he stood, he bounced himself back and forth looking nervously into the dark.

"Well," the man said in low voice after a long time of thought, "do you have a place where you can spend the night?"

"No," Alexandra exclaimed.

"There is an empty room where I live," the man muttered timidly. "If you want, I can take you there to spend the night."

They gazed rapidly at each other in tacit agreement. This was their only chance. It was either to trust the strange fellow that had approached them or spend the night on the street.

"Thanks, we'll go with you." Mariana said. They got their luggage and followed him into the car.

My name is Jack, Jack Morris," he said as he put the luggage inside the car. "I live close by, only a few minutes away." His voice was louder, possessed by a sudden happiness.

Alexandra's heart was pounding madly. She knew her sister's and friend's was too. The man sped away. In five minutes he reached Fulton Street, went up four more streets, then turned right. Each minute seemed to have enlarged into eternal lapses to Alexandra. What will happen now? She wondered uneasily. Her sister and friend were quiet, petrified with fear like she was.

Suddenly, the car stopped.

"It's here," the man said, jumping out of the car and letting them out as he pointed at an old, dirty building. The street was full of garbage, and the building seemed abandoned. Graffiti covered the walls along the street.

He opened the door slowly and they followed him in. Inside the building, everything was dark. A very dim light at the top of the stairs illuminated the hallway. The paint was peeling off the walls and big chunks of wood were missing on the staircase. The man began to climb. They tried to climb silently, but decayed wood squeaked at their feet.

When they reached the third floor the man stopped in front of an open door on the right side.

"This is it," he said, walking into the room. "The apartment has been empty for two weeks. I live across this hall. I hope this helps you; I'm going to sleep now". He deposited the luggage on the floor and left as mysteriously as he had appeared, closing the door timidly and leaving them in total darkness, except for the pale rays of the moon that filtrated inside the room through the broken windows.

They sat on the floor in dreadful silence and looked around. There was no furniture. It was bare, dirty, and it seemed almost impossible that someone actually could have lived there in such decrepit conditions two weeks ago. The floor was cluttered with garbage, clusters of cockroaches climbed on the wall, and two rats were standing on top of a deteriorated stove stuck in one corner.

"We have to get out of here as soon as possible," Alexandra whispered, looking at the rats that from time to time interrupted what they were eating on the stove to look at them.

"It is my fault," Hilda blamed herself dolefully. "If I only hadn't talked to him--but what else could I have done if we were in his house and he kept talking to me?"

"Shut up," Mariana answered. "It wasn't your fault. You weren't flirting with him. He liked you and the woman noticed it--everybody noticed it."

"She is right," Alexandra replied. "He liked you the moment he saw you. It's not your fault."

"Well, for whatever reason we are here now, in this ugly place. I'm scared," Hilda said.

"We are too," Mariana replied.

They spent the rest of the night sitting and listening to every little sound.

29

They spent five nights in that building until they got paid and were able to rent an apartment. The man in the car found the apartment. He was a friend of the superintendent of a nearby apartment building, and at his request, "the super" had agreed to rent them an apartment. The neighborhood was awful, but this apartment building, compared to the one they had been in for the last five days, was a palace. It was in much better condition, not as dark, and a little less deteriorated. The subway entrance was at the corner, and it was located in a more populated zone.

They breathed with relief for the first time in two and a half weeks after they signed the monthly arrangement with "the super."

The apartment was on the fourth floor. It had big windows that faced to the west, and a large room that functioned as bedroom as well as living room. It also had a separate bathroom with a shower, and a kitchen.

"Wow!" they exclaimed after they moved in, laughing loudly, letting escape the tension of the scary moments of the past.

"I am going to buy some food to put something in our refrigerator and in our stomachs. I saw a store on the corner when Jack drove us here," said Alexandra as she got her purse and walked with confidence towards the door.

"O.K." She heard her sister say as she closed the door and headed quickly downstairs.

As she had seen in Bridge City, in this part of Brooklyn there were only blacks on the street. Alexandra didn't care. She was in love with a black man—madly in love about him.

She arrived to the store in the best of spirits, ignoring the curiosity that her presence had caused inside the store. She bought her groceries, paid the bill and happily walked out. She felt grateful that God had protected them. Something very wrong could have happened to them, but they had been preserved.

Unexpectedly, a handful of stones and garbage fell over her.

"GET OUT of here you fucking son of a bitch white bitch, we don't want you here!"

Alexandra looked about. Seven black girls standing outside a building door glared at her threateningly.

Here we go again, one more racial confrontation, Alexandra thought. She kept walking naturally as if they hadn't just attacked her with the stones, and passed by them as they continued to berate her with all sorts of insulting and derogatory remarks.

Human condition cannot be disguised, she thought pitifully as more garbage fell on her back. It always comes out like a brutal and blunt revelation in the way people move, talk, and in the things they do. It is sad, because the real liberation and emancipation come from within, from what people think about themselves, and not from what others say about them.

As she reached the apartment building, she went upstairs slowly. All of a sudden she felt weary, as if she were carrying a heavy weight and suddenly was overcome by it. She opened the door unhurriedly and stepped in.

"What happened?" Mariana asked. She and Hilda were washing off the last remains of grease on the kitchen walls.

"Nothing," Alexandra said dismally, sitting down.

"Don't lie. You looked as if you have seen the very devil."

Alexandra raised her shoulders. "In a way I did," she answered. "Some black girls threw rocks at me near the corner. The rocks didn't really hurt me as much as their words. It is depressing."

"What did they say?" Hilda asked.

"All sort of insulting remarks. You don't want to know."

"It is a natural reaction to the oppression and exploitation they have experienced for so long," Mariana said in a conciliatory manner.

"The blacks have been so cruelly mistreated and abused in this country, that they want somehow to show their resentment." Hilda added.

"I guess what you say is true," Alexandra said, "but violence doesn't solve the problem. It only augments it. War only brings war, and in war, oftentimes the innocent pay for the sinners."

Mariana and Hilda agreed.

"Well, what are we going to do now?" Hilda asked.

"Nothing, we are here," Alexandra concluded. "We have to make the best of it until we can move to Manhattan."

They cooked, ate, and set the apartment in order, while they listened to the pleasing voice of Billie Holiday.

"Well, girls, we have had the busiest day," Mariana remarked. "Bed time."

They laughed and began to undress. Suddenly Mariana screamed.

"Look!" she exclaimed, pointing at the window. The color had left her cheeks.

Four black men who had climbed up the fire escape were staring at them with lascivious eyes. It was obvious that they had seen them naked. They covered themselves with their robes and without thinking further they stormed out of the apartment.

"Let's ask the super to call the police," Mariana said.

They made so much noise going downstairs that several tenants who were already in bed came out to find out who was causing that kind of turmoil.

"Mr. Jackson, open the door, please hurry!" Alexandra called, banging at the door.

A very sleepy Mr. Jackson opened the door.

"What's going on, girls? What's all this racket?"

"There were four men standing outside our windows on the fire escape. Perhaps they would have gotten in while we were asleep, if Mariana had not seen them." Hilda said. Her mouth was dry and she was very pale. "Can you go with us to check the apartment, and can you call the police? We don't have a phone yet and we are scared."

The superintendent remained thoughtful for a few seconds. He was a huge black man. His hair was absolutely white, and his face had an unusual suavity.

"One moment, please," he said as he walked back into his bedroom.

A few minutes later when he came back to the door he was carrying an iron stick in his hand.

"All right, girls," he said firmly, "I am ready."

"We have to get out of here as soon as possible," Alexandra whispered in Mariana's ear. "Tomorrow we might not be so lucky."

"You are right," Mariana admitted as they went upstairs.

The men weren't at the fire escape anymore, but everyone in the building had come out of their apartments awakened by the screams.

"This neighborhood is not for you girls," the super said. "You need to move. I mean it." He went through every room in the apartment with the iron stick in his hand.

"Nope," he repeated more to himself than to them. "They are not here." He secured the windows once more, then left the apartment. "Don't forget what I've told you. You need to move. Goodnight."

Alexandra, Mariana, and Hilda guarded the windows the rest of the night, much too excited and scared to relax. As soon as the morning came, they headed to Manhattan on the morning rush hour train. Mr. Boudreaux was their only recourse. They had no money. What little money they had, they had spent in paying the rent for the apartment to which they could no longer go. Those black men, whoever they were, knew that they were alone, and if they didn't get them that night inside the building, they could very well get them on the streets. This was a black neighborhood. As whites, they were the intruders and their presence wasn't welcome.

30

Mr. Boudreaux was behind his desk giving orders to some people when he saw them. He waved to them with cheer, and as soon as he finished his conversation, he stepped out of his office to greet them.

"Girls, girls, what a surprise! I've been so worried about you. Come, to my office," he said, as he kissed them and held them one by one with that frankness of his that made him so likeable. "It's so good to see you."

Alexandra, Mariana, and Hilda followed him in silence.

"Please sit down," he said, "My uncle told me what happened. I am very sorry. What are you going to do now?"

"This is why we came to see you," Mariana said. "We have no where to stay." And in a few words she related to him what had happened to them since the time they left his uncle's house.

"Girls, girls, what am I going to do with you?" he teased, but the frown on his face betrayed his real feelings of worry. "Well," he said after a moment of thought, rubbing his chin with his right hand, "I'll talk with some friends about your situation and will let you know later what I can do for you. Come back after work. I will have some options for you by then." He stood up as he glanced at his watch. "I have a meeting to attend, but don't worry, leave things up to me. Go get some lunch, take a walk on Fifth Avenue, and come see me later. Everything will be all right, you'll see."

They stood up, kissed him goodbye, and headed back to the elevator.

"Girls, wait!" Franz Boudreaux was behind them. "Take this," he said, extracting a fifty-dollar bill out of his pocket. "You need it."

"Franz, we can't--" Alexandra began.

"Please, take it," he said. "You'll pay me when you can. I don't need it now, you do." And with that, he turned around, leaving them speechless and grateful in front of the elevator.

At the end of the day as Franz had asked them to do, they went back to his office. It was 4:45 p.m. They were fifteen minutes early, so they sat in the elegant reception area to wait. They had gone around town, visited Central Park, fed the ducks and flocks of doves that gathered everywhere in the park, but what they hadn't been able to do was ease their nervousness. The closer the clock moved to five, the more nervous they became.

"Hello, my friends, good to see you," Mr. Boudreaux said, his cane and hat in hand as he approached them. "I have good news for you. I have some friends on 72nd Street--that's where you will be able to stay. Cheer up! C'mon, smile!"

They started laughing. Franz Boudreaux's joy for life was contagious, so contagious that Alexandra started to cry, as she always did when she felt the genuine power and beauty of human nature.

31

The apartment on 72nd Street was modern and pretty. It consisted of two floors and was located in a bohemian area, similar to Greenwich Village, where extravagant and eccentric people gathered to protest the conventionalisms of a deranged society.

Mr. Boudreaux's friends were two bachelor brothers. One appeared to be around forty years old, and the other around twenty-five. They were also from Haiti, but only their wavy black hair showed any traces of their ancestry. The color of their skin and features were that of whites, and judging by the exquisite decoration of the apartment and the expensive clothes they were wearing, they were affluent.

As Franz spoke to introduce them, the forty-year-old smoked his pipe. He was sitting in front of them, and as he smoked, his eyes ran up and down over Alexandra's body, who tried to appear calm despite the enormous nervousness she felt. The younger brother was standing a few steps behind the piano listening attentively to what Franz and his brother were saying. It was obvious by the attitude of the younger that the older brother made the decisions there.

"Of course they can stay here, Franz. This is a good area. Everything is near--the supermarket, downtown, the subway. Living here will make it easier for them to look for an apartment in Manhattan."

"Merci, mon chere," Mr. Boudreaux said, gratefully.

"Pas de quois, mon frere. Pas de quois."

They stood up, hugged amicably, and together walked to the door.

"Bye, girls." Franz waved when he reached the door. "Let me know how everything progresses."

"We will, thanks." Alexandra shouted. They all sighed as Franz disappeared behind the door.

The forty year old came towards them.

"My brother and I aren't at home much during the day," he explained. "My brother goes to school, and I work. Come," he added, taking Alexandra's hand with familiarity, "I will show you the bedrooms."

A well-crafted winding staircase in the east corner of the living room connected to the second floor where the bedrooms were.

"We have three bedrooms here," he explained. "This is my brother's, this is mine, and this one is for our guests. From now on until the day you are ready to move from our place, this will be your bedroom."

The bedroom was a pretty good size. In the middle of the room there was an inviting queen size bed with a blue satin quilt. An enormous portrait of a lion's face handcrafted with enchanting workmanship hung on one of the walls. A dresser with gardenias, an exquisite lamp, and five gigantic pillows in different tones of blue were scattered on the cushioned carpet. Whoever decorated this apartment did it with finesse, Alexandra thought.

"These are the house keys." The forty-year-old man was saying. "One opens the front door and this other one opens the apartment."

"Thanks for your hospitality," Mariana said.

"You are welcome. Call me Ralph, my brother's name is Loui." He turned to the door and left the room, leaving behind the aroma of his expensive lotion.

"Now what?" Hilda asked.

"We'll see." Alexandra responded, shrugging.

"He likes you," Mariana noted. "He likes you a lot. I hope we don't have problems."

Alexandra shivered lightly. It hadn't been hard for them to notice Ralph's fervent glances. She bit her lips nervously as she hoped silently that they wouldn't have any more problems of that sort.

32

They spent the next six days without eventualities, except for Ralph's eyes that followed Alexandra everywhere she went. It was uncomfortable. She had avoided him, until the seventh day, when she got home from shopping and found Ralph at home.

"Hi," she greeted when she saw him.

"Hi," he answered hoarsely, coming towards her. He had a glass of wine in his hand and as he followed her into the kitchen, Alexandra had a very uneasy sensation.

"Where is my sister, and Hilda?" she asked apprehensively as she deposited the groceries that she was carrying on the kitchen table.

"They aren't home," he answered, coming closer. "We are alone."

Ralph was almost over her. Alexandra had seen eyes like those before in Thomas' eyes, and had heard that rasping tone of voice.

"Alexandra.." He accosted her in the kitchen. He was sweaty and trembling. "You don't have to move from here when your sisters move; you can stay here with me." He snatched her into his arms. "I can cover you with gold. I have wanted you since the moment I saw you." He was striving to rob her kisses. "I'll buy you anything you want. I'll let you do anything you want to do. If you want to go to school, I'll pay for the tuition. I will give you jewels, clothes, perfumes, anything you ask me--anything you want for a moment of your body..."

"I am not for sale," Alexandra shouted, offended. She tried to release herself from the arms that were clamping her so tightly and immobilizing her body. "Who do you think I am? Let go of me--you are hurting me!"

"Everyone has a price," he said, pinning her against the wall. "Look, look at this." He took from his pocket two handfuls of hundred dollar bills and thrust them in her hand. "I can give you anything you want, just remember that. Anything!"

"Stop it!" she screamed, throwing the money on the floor. "Can't you tell that no matter how much you give me you can't have me? I am not for sale!"

He looked at her for a moment, then, released her hastily. Her sister and Hilda had unexpectedly come in.

"Think it over," he whispered, wiping the sweat of his face and regaining his composure. "I will be waiting for your answer." He passed by Mariana and Hilda, who, ignorant of what had just happened, were laughing gaily. He greeted them formally, then stormed out of the apartment, infuriated and defeated.

"What's up with him?" Mariana asked. "He seems a little bit uptight. What happened here?" she asked once more, looking at the hundred dollar bills that were still scattered on the floor.

"He wants to trade our shelter for my body, that's what happened!" Alexandra said, still crushed. "No one can give anything without having an ulterior motive."

"Calm down," Mariana said. "Take it easy!"

Alexandra stared at her sister. Of the three, Mariana was the one who always kept cool. She had the ability to put her head before her heart, especially in situations like this one.

Mariana was very attractive. Her black hair and skin showed the influence of the Moors. There was no surprise about that, her father always said, not in vain had the Moors conquered and dominated Spain for over five hundred years. When they left, not only had they left monuments and traces of their magnificent culture but of their physical appearance as well.

"We have to move," Mariana continued after thinking for a while. She had a pencil in her hand, and as she spoke, she was scribbling on a piece of paper, glancing at Alexandra, Hilda, and the money that remained spread on the floor. "We can't do it right now. We don't get paid until tomorrow, but even then, we can't move until we find an apartment."

"We can look for one on the weekend, and if we are lucky, we will find one," Hilda said." Then we can move right away."

Alexandra stood up; she picked up the money that was scattered on the floor, put it inside an envelope, and went upstairs to drop it on Ralph's bedroom floor. She was still fuming over his offensive words. Only a few people were like Franz Boudreaux, or like the Brooklyn stranger. As far as Ralph Dominique, it was obvious that he was used to getting everything he wanted with money.

She walked towards the bedroom dresser, got the phone and dialed Jules's number. She hadn't heard from him since she left New Orleans. She had sent him a letter but had asked him not to write until she had a permanent address...At the other end of the line, she heard his voice.

"Hello? Jules speaking."

"Hi," Alexandra stammered, almost out of breath. All of a sudden, her body was shaking with uncontrollable emotion. "This is Alexandra. How are you doing?"

"Alexandra, what a surprise!" he said. "My sister is in New York. She moved up there after she lost her baby." He paused for a second. "She was very depressed after that happened, so she decided to move away from here."

"I am very sorry to hear that. It's awful!" Alexandra exclaimed.

"I can give you her address if you want so you can go visit her. It will be good for her. She will be very happy to see you; she likes you."

"Thank you, I like her very much too."

"Do you have a pencil ready?" he asked.

"Yes, I do."

She noted the address happily. "Did you say apartment 300?"

"Yes." Jules answered. "Have you guys an address of your own?"

"No, not yet, but soon." She said shortly.

"Well, good luck then. Write soon, and let me know if you see my sister."

"I will. Thanks...Bye."

"Bye."

Still shaking, Alexandra hung up the phone and ran downstairs.

"Guess what happened?" she screamed with excitement as she entered the living room.

"What's going on? Have you gone crazy?" Mariana asked.

"Bella is here. In New York!" Alexandra replied excitedly. "She can help us to find an apartment, and if we ask her she might let us stay with her for the time it takes us to find an apartment of our own. I don't want to stay here one more minute. Well, no longer than tomorrow. It is too dangerous."

"Yes, it is." Hilda agreed.

"Wow! This is great news!" Mariana said. "God is good to us; when we most need Him, He always helps us!"

33

Alexandra had to go to work that evening, but instead of catching the train, she decided to walk. It was a long walk, but it didn't matter. Her spirits after talking to Jules were high, life was beautiful, and she felt alive, able, and capable of conquering anything.

Ralph's actions that afternoon didn't bother her anymore. She hadn't lost anything. He had. During his forty years, along the way, he hadn't learned to be a gentleman. A new change was coming into their lives, she could tell--perhaps it would come after they met with Bella.

In this section of town the prostitutes were standing on every corner. They were young and old, black and white. As she passed by them, Alexandra didn't look at them with disdain, but with consideration and regard. Only tragedy and abuse could have brought them where they were. Their heavy makeup was perhaps their disguise, their frivolous outfits the masks of sensitive hearts. Perhaps once in their lives they had met crooked men like Ralph Dominique who had made them instruments of their perversions, or perhaps they were the result of the patriarchal, uncaring, and brutal system that most of the time benefited and pardoned the abuser, and punished and oppressed the needy.

Her reflections ended abruptly when she arrived at the luxurious hotel to start another evening's work.

"How do you do?" She greeted the porter with a bright smile then, walked to the front desk to take her post.

34

"Child, what a surprise!" Bella exclaimed gleefully embracing her. "Come in, please, come in. These are..?" she raised her left eyebrow as she switched her eyes from Mariana to Hilda.

"I am Mariana, Alexandra's sister."

"I am Hilda, Their friend."

"Oh, good to meet you!" Bella greeted, embracing them too. "Please sit down. Who would have known that we all would gather here in New York?"

"Yes, indeed." Alexandra said.

"I lost my baby child," Bella moaned. "They waited too long to induce labor and the baby was born dead." Tears were pouring down her face. "I am sorry," she apologized, taking hold of a handkerchief, "but it was so sad. It was a boy. You should have seen him; he was so beautiful."

Bella quietly looked destroyed, unable to get over the horrid recollection of her experience. The weight of Bella's pain couldn't be tempered.

"Well, tell me," she said after a few minutes of crying. "What's up with you? Where do you guys live? Have you found a place yet?"

"As a matter of fact, we are still looking for a place. Do you know of any around the neighborhood?"

"I certainly do!" Bella said with sudden enthusiasm. "There is an empty apartment on the next floor. The manager is very nice; we could go talk to him right now. He lives on the main floor."

They gazed at each other in awe. There was no doubt that this was their lucky day, and that Providence was one more time providing for their welfare.

"Would you do that for us?" Alexandra asked.

"Let's go, then," Bella said as she walked towards a nearby mirror, combing with her hand the hair that had fallen in jumbles over her face when she was crying.

"I look horrible, but who cares. Let's go."

35

You don't have to move," Ralph Dominique said, holding Alexandra by the arm with force when he saw them taking their things out of the apartment. His dark eyes behind the thick eyelashes had an expression of disbelief combined with fury.

He had been drinking, and though not drunk yet, he had lost all decorum.

"You don't need to move with them," he repeated, pressing close to her ear, "Look," he added as he grasped with his free hand one of the four bottles of perfume that he had lined up on the living room table. "I can buy you perfumes like these." he squirted Alexandra's body up and down with one aroma, ignoring the astonished glances of Mariana and Hilda, who were standing close to them. "I'll do anything you want; I'll give you anything you want, if you let me see your body!"

Alexandra pulled back and blushed.

"Let's go," she said to Mariana and Hilda, ignoring Ralph.

They went towards the door. They opened it and closed it quickly behind them as the disdainful voice of Ralph said, "You know where I live if you change your mind. I'll be waiting for you!"

36

In the east the sun was rising, bringing the city to life.

Alexandra ran excitedly downstairs, not wanting to miss the sun's awakening. Since they had moved to Bella's building six months ago, she had made it a habit to walk in Central Park every morning at sunrise. At that time of the morning, Central Park was absolutely beautiful. It provided a quiet and strange refuge in the midst of the tumultuous and disruptive rush of the city.

"Hi child, did you know that Jules is here?" Bella whispered softly in her ear when she met her at the elevator door. "He got here so late last night that we didn't have time to let you know.

Willie and I have to work this morning, but you can come by to see him." Her eyes were smiling as they left the elevator. "He'll be there."

"Yes, I will. Thanks," Alexandra said, almost voiceless as she stopped near the front door. She was on her way out to see the sunlight, but suddenly another sunlight, dear to her heart, was just a few doors away from her arms.

She didn't wait for the elevator, but covered the three flights running. Her heart was pounding so madly that it hurt intensely inside her chest. Trembling, with no other thought in mind but the need to see him, she knocked at Bella's apartment door.

"Hi," she said, blushing, and she fell prisoner to that burning spell that pulled her so strongly towards Jules.

"Hi," Jules said without surprise. "Come in."

He had a blue robe covering his body, and in his eyes that inexpressive look of his, so hard to unravel that it enervated her.

She stepped in shyly, holding her breath. If Jules was glad to see her, it didn't show. As soon as she stepped in, he went back into the bedroom without uttering a word, then back to his temporary bed.

She didn't know why, but when she saw his reaction, the smile she had on her face froze, and an awkward sensation took hold of her body. All of a sudden all she wanted to do was to run and to hide. But Alexandra's body, contrary to her desires, didn't move; her feet seemed to be screwed to the floor. A deep shame overtook her, and in the silence, the loud hammering of her heart seemed to expose her bewilderment. Can Jules tell how humiliated I feel? She thought. Alexandra couldn't tell, but the silent moment was building her self-doubt. After a while of uncertainty, Alexandra began to move her feet slowly.

The light inside Jules' bedroom was dim. Heavy blue drapes covered the two windows and it was hard to see clearly. She moved a little closer to the bed. On the bed, Jules was clothed with the covers. His eyes were closed. She sat on the side of the bed close to where Jules' arms were. Since the first time they made love together, she didn't know what he thought about her, what he felt for her. Ever since then, his eyes had remained away from hers avoiding the encounter of her look.

She didn't know how long she stayed in repose at the side of the bed, watching his sleep. His skin was amazingly dark and attractive, and just looking at him, he inflamed her heart. Slowly, she took the covers off his body and began to caress him.

"I love you." Alexandra said fervently. But lying there, he was just a static statue of ebony that she couldn't bring to life.

"The woman I marry," Jules said abruptly, "will have the respect of my friends. If you didn't get any respect from Thomas when you were in Mexico, it is because your behavior with him must not have inspired it. I can't marry one who has been offering herself to my friends." The expression of his eyes darkened to rage. You let him kissed you," he went on. "If you wouldn't have provoked him, he wouldn't have done it. "There is more than one way for a woman to prostitute herself than just to have sex with a man."

"Why are you doing this to me? I did nothing wrong."

"He kissed you!" he said implacable, "isn't that enough?"

Two days later, Jules left. At the airport, Bella, Willie, and herself embraced Jules in goodbye. She waved at him until Jules' figure had gone beyond her eyes' reach, lost in the crowd. She contained her tears. Today, like the day she left New Orleans, she didn't know where she really stood in Jules' heart. He had left her again in a dubious and agonizing suspense.

In time things will work out, she thought.

37

Incited by Jules' silence, without any further thought, the next free weekend Alexandra had, she flew to New Orleans. Four months had passed since Jules came to New York, made love to her, left, and she couldn't take anymore that silence. She needed to see him, to hold him, and to hear what he felt about her.

New Orleans hadn't changed. It was always hot, sunny, and humid. She breathed deeply--there was no question that this was a beautiful part of the country.

"Loyola University, please," she said, getting into the taxi.

"Right on," the taxi driver said as he sped up along the streets to her desired destination.

Thrilled with anticipation and memories, she let her eyes wander. It had been a year and a half since the first time she was there. The establishment's windows no longer carried dehumanizing messages separating blacks from whites. It was rejoicing to be a step farther ahead towards the solution of race inequality, a problem that had risen only through ignorance, abuse, and misconception. The taxi parked in front of the main University entrance and Alexandra got out. She paid the fare rapidly and ran across the campus. She couldn't wait to see him. She loved him and was hopeful to make things work out between them.

"Is Jules here?" she questioned as she opened the glass door, catching her breath.

The receptionist looked at her. "Yes, he is. Four doors to the right."

Alexandra rushed straight in. Suddenly, she came to a halt outside his office. Inside, Jules was kissing a woman passionately. Without knowing what else to do, Alexandra stood outside the office door, paralyzed by anguish. Finally, noticing her presence, the woman and Jules stopped kissing.

"Well, darling," the woman said with an English accent, as she kissed Jules again, briefly. "I'll see you later." She glanced at Alexandra with curiosity as she passed by her.

"O.K." Jules answered, then turned to face Alexandra. "Hi," he said naturally, as if he had seen her the day before, and it didn't make any difference that she had found him in the arms of that woman.

"Hi," Alexandra said with a strange voice, feeling a sudden shame.

"What hotel are you staying in?" he asked, turning his back on her as he arranged some papers on his desk."

"I don't have a place to stay. I just arrived," she answered, disturbed, then, added with a trembling voice, "who is she?"

He stopped for a moment what he was doing. "Her name is Darla. She is my lady friend; she is from England." He looked at his watch, got his checkbook out of the drawer, and ignoring Alexandra, he walked towards the door. "I have to go to lunch," he said, "I am running a little late this afternoon. I finish work at five o'clock; if you don't have a place to stay, I can take you with me to Bridge City. You can stay in the house where you stayed with my sister when she used to live here. The house is still empty." Having said that, he stepped out and disappeared behind the office door without giving her the opportunity to answer.

She was so shocked with his disinterest that she had to sit down to recover. Jules no longer loved her. Her relationship with him was nothing but a folly. She left his office and wandered in the city all day like a zombie, and at five o'clock, despite her conclusions, she came back to his office carrying with her the inexplicable and overtaking desire to see him for at least another minute, another instant, even if that instant or minute would lead to a life of hell.

After five minutes wait, Jules strode out of his office, passed by her ignoring her presence, and exited though the door. Biting her lips with painful distress, Alexandra stood up and followed after him. Apparently he was walking very fast, because the few seconds she had taken to go after him, had given him more than a few yards lead. He was clearly annoyed, as though he had purposely tried to leave her behind to show her that her presence wasn't wanted.

"Wait!" she called, running after him, as if she hadn't sensed his resistance.

"Hurry!" he said, turning for an instant to see her, "I am late to pick up Darla." He got inside his car and slammed the door.

Alexandra ran to catch up with him, opened the passenger door and sat down, fatigued as a very impatient Jules released the brakes of his car. He sped up around the campus, reached Tulane University library without saying a word, and parked his blue Cadillac violently with a loud squeak. He was visibly impatient; he kept on looking at his watch every other minute as his right hand continuously tapped the wheel.

It was only after a few minutes wait that Darla came out from the library. She was smiling, like she had been smiling when Jules kissed her a few hours ago in his office. She was very pretty, almost too pretty and gracious. She carried herself with bearing, yet without conceit. Her curly chestnut hair streamed down her shoulders, and her eyes, the color of sapphires, had a kind look.

Alexandra's heart was hurting.

As soon as Jules caught sight of her, he became elated. He jumped out of the car without delay, and ran towards her. They met half way on the stairs, and there they held and kissed, ignoring Alexandra and the world.

"Hi," Darla greeted Alexandra, getting inside Jules' car. "Jules told me that he met you in Mexico City. Is that so?"

"Yes," Alexandra answered, trying to hide her humiliation, but her voice, came out as a hollow groan.

No one said one more word. They drove in silence for the next seven minutes until Darla suddenly laughed.

"It's here, Jules! Don't you remember?"

"Pardon me," Jules answered, stopping the car abruptly. "I wasn't thinking. I'll be back in a minute," he said addressing Alexandra as he opened the car's door and held Darla by the hand to help her get off the car.

Those tears that always betrayed Alexandra came out, burning her eyes. Across the street the one to whom she had given her body and her soul was kissing Darla as if she had never existed in his life.

How different was her relationship with Jules than the way she had imagined. Her young hopes and dreams of love had all crashed against Jules' indifference. She dashed out of the car and began to run down one street after another in an effort to get as far as possible from what was hurting her so badly. As she ran, she wiped her tears with her hand. His disrespect, more than his indifference, was more than she could handle.

It was dark. The sun, at this time of the year, set early in New Orleans. She ran until she gasped for breath, then slowly, walked back to Loyola University. Tired and overheated as she was, she found a drinking fountain, and drank with pressing need, splashing her face and hair with the refreshing water again and again. She had never smoked, but at that moment, persuaded that nothing mattered anymore, she deposited some quarters and got two packs of cigarettes from the dispenser. She smoked one cigarette after another, choking and coughing without knowing where to go or what to do. All of a sudden the world was a miserable, lonely, rotten place in which honesty was always taken for a ride.

Some students passed by and stared at her, baffled. She was dressed with expensive clothes that flattered her figure and her wet hair fell over her shoulders like a dark gold mantle. She was still smoking. Perhaps at first glance, the students sensed, that her conduct did not correspond with her appearance. She shook her head in an attempt to regain poise despite the impertinent looks, and began to walk towards the student lounge. Jules' rejection had hurt her pride immensely, but for some reason, it had also increased the impulse of her feelings: she loved him and needed him. It was hard to understand why precisely now when she had seen him with another woman and received from him nothing but disdain.

In the lounge, some students chatted as others watched a movie. Quietly, Alexandra sat down in one of the corners of the spacious room.

At twelve midnight, Jules stood in front of her like a judge.

"Why did you run away?" His dispassionate manner was gone--he was profoundly upset. "I've been looking for you all over."

Alexandra looked at him in surprise. He had such a concerned, angry look in his eyes and such a horrid frown that she broke into laughter.

"Are you crazy?" He said, taking her roughly by the arms and shaking her.

She stopped laughing as she inhaled her cigarette and deliberately exhaled the smoke slowly into his face.

"I didn't know you smoke." He said, irritated.

"I didn't know either." She laughed, pretending to be loose and frivolous.

"I am going back to Bridge City. Are you coming with me or not?" He began to walk away.

Alexandra followed him, still laughing.

Far from the romance I had expected, Alexandra thought while Jules rode to Bridge City in absolute and willful silence. The whole situation was suddenly amusing and ironic. While she had given Jules her devotion, he had given his to another woman. Glancing at his profile sideways from her seat, Jules appeared extremely funny. Not knowing why, she felt inclined to sing, and so she did. First low, like a whisper, then with feeling, pouring her soul into the romantic song.

"Shut up!" Jules erupted. "You don't know how to sing." He could hardly breath from exasperation.

Alexandra ignored Jules' outburst and continued to sing "Misty." Her eyes were fixed on him with all the reproach that her soul felt at that moment.

When they got in front of what had been his sister's house in Bridge City, he stopped the car.

"Get out!" he demanded, opening the car door. "The front door is open. There is a bed in there. There is no electricity." His face was contorted with anger. He went back to his car, slammed the door, and disappeared on the corner as he turned left, heading to his house.

Alexandra stood in the middle of the dirt road listening to the crickets that were the only witness of her misery. Then, walking slowly, she went inside the house. As she opened the door, the door squeaked with a desolate sound and she found herself alone inside. The rays of the silvery moon were there, as faithfully as the first time she had been in that house, coming through the windowpane. She plucked the pack of cigarettes from her purse and, smiling with regret, dumped it in the garbage.

38

She woke up early in the morning and walked to Jules' house. It was Saturday and he didn't work. She rang the bell, and Jules, upon opening the door, was not a bit surprised to see her. He seemed to have been expecting her.

"I have to go for a few hours to New Orleans, but you can stay here if you want," he invited with friendly voice. He seemed changed; his face showed no signs of his earlier anger.

"Yes, I'll stay," she said.

"All right, then. It won't take me that long. I'll see you in a little while," Jules said.

"Bye."

Immediately, as he left, Alexandra went directly to Jules' bedroom. She was alone in the house. The black ladies who lived with Jules had gone to Baton Rouge to visit a friend, Jules had mentioned, and at this moment, nothing sounded more pleasing to her than to be alone.

She looked around. The house was very modest, but clean. Jules's bed was neatly made. The books in the bookcase were in perfect order; the dresser was immaculate. There was no sign of dust anywhere. Everything in the bedroom showed his meticulous side. As her eyes scanned the room, they stopped on the small bureau he had at one side of his bed. Her heart trembled. The photograph that they had taken in Mexico together was still there.

What hypocrisy, Alexandra thought. This is absolutely unbelievable.

She selected one of his books and carelessly climbed on the bed to begin reading it, when a brown sack at one side of the bed caught her attention. It was a paper shopping bag full of letters. Alexandra shuffled them, took a handful of them and began to read one letter after another...until she felt an immense nausea.

"No!" She threw the letters aside. "It's not possible! This can't be possible!"

The letters, scattered over the quilt, were written testimonies of Jules' dishonesty. Frantically, she took the sack and dumped the rest of the letters on the bed. There were at least two hundred.

Alexandra had only read twelve, but each, had been from a woman that was in love with Jules. Each was from a woman that was in distress because he hadn't replied to her letters, each from a woman that had had his baby. Jules had condemned her for her disloyalty with Thomas, and he had been and was the most deceitful. Feeling almost insane, she took the little picture that Jules had kept over the bureau as a token of the love he had promised to her, and ripped it into a million pieces. Then, she got the scissors, and in frenzy, she cut the thick locks of her hair until she left her head almost bald. No tears fell from her eyes. Her mouth was dry; she felt dizzy and filled with grief.

No longer able to contain her disgust, she walked out of the house tumbling, reached the wooden bathroom that was a few yards away from the house, and vomited in the hole. The repulse she felt was unbearable. As she came back into the house, she saw that Jules had returned. He was standing in the middle of his bedroom, looking with astonished eyes at the letters over the bed, and the hair over the floor. He was pale. She went directly towards him and started to hit him, unable to control her fury.

"You are the most miserable, the most dishonest, the most dirty, the most immoral, the most..." She couldn't continue. "Why didn't you tell me that your style is to have kids everywhere?" she cried. "It is sickening!"

"You had no business digging in my things," he said vehemently, picking up the letters that were scattered over the bed and putting them back into the sack. "Even spouses don't tell one another everything. I was planning on marrying you and I considered that this was not a thing I wanted you to know."

"You are so revolting, shameful and ignoble. I still can't believe that you could be like this, and could willingly hurt so many women."

She wanted to die, and wished he would become angry enough to strike her in the heart to end the insufferable and exorbitant pain she felt, and let her forget his duplicity.

He held her in his arms and she fell on her knees, incapable of restraining the weakness and desire that ripened in her as she knelt at his side.

"I am going to leave tomorrow," she murmured, weeping grievously. She couldn't talk anymore. He was covering her body with his.

The following morning she left New Orleans, aghast. She was running away from the strange and mysterious fascination that Jules exercised on her despite the sordid things that she had learned about him.

39

Back in New York, things seemed to be normal, but they weren't. Hilda, broken to pieces, had gone back to Mexico after she found out she was pregnant, and her boyfriend, with cold disinterest, had asked her to abort.

As for Alexandra's sister, she had gone to live with her boyfriend. Alexandra was the only one living in the apartment that the three had shared.

The sound of the telephone startled her. She had been sitting in the living room, lights dimmed, listening to the music of Bach, with her soul haunted by tormenting memories.

"Hello?"

"Child, I was just thinking that you should come to live with us," Bella said. "We have a big apartment and this way you wouldn't be alone, you see."

"Thanks, Bella. Let me think about it."

"O.K., child. Take your time, but don't take too long, all right? We want to help you." Bella said.

"I know. Thanks"

"Let us know when you are ready to move, O.K.?"

"I will, thanks again. Bye"

After Bella hung up. Alexandra began to undress, turned the light off, and went to bed. She didn't want to think or remember. It was better to be without feeling, that way it didn't hurt so much. She closed her eyes.

40

To get a job as a telephone operator or front desk clerk in New York was rather easy. It was crazy for anyone to want to deal all day with so many crazy people demanding crazy things in an already crazy world, but not for Alexandra. She had two jobs. It was a fast pace life, but people's problems took her away from her own. She left one place of work and started immediately at the other. No change, but that night when she came home, she was in for a surprise--she found the letter at the door. Her father had died in the midst of his last adventure. One winter morning, someone had found him lying on the side of the street dead.

Far and away from everything and everyone that had been dear to him, her father's spirit had finally quit enslaved by alcohol. Under its malefic influence, he had not hesitated to give up all. The chilling reward of his vice had been his horrific death, and the misery and disastrous consequences he had brought with it to his wife and his seven children.

Alexandra read the news in silence and couldn't cry. The childhood night of terror ended there with the macabre passing of her father. In Mexico City, her youngest brother had received the notice from the coroner to go to Guadalajara to identify the body that rested in the City Morgue, after the required autopsy for unclaimed corpses had been performed.

41

At Bella's house, Alexandra felt at home. Bella always talked about Jules, and when she did, Alexandra wondered how things would have been between them had Thomas not interfered in their affairs. Despite these bothersome questions, for the first time in weeks, everything seemed to be in order. She had nothing to worry about, in Bella's house, she felt protected and secure. But that morning, when Bella went to work, Bella's husband slipped very quietly into Alexandra's bedroom. She was still asleep and didn't notice his presence. Not until she felt someone caressing her face did she wake up, startled.

"Shh...shh," Willie said innocently, putting a finger across his lips. "Don't be frightened, Alexandra, it's only me." He was smiling idiotically.

"What do you want?" Alexandra said defensively, rising up and covering herself with the blanket. "Why didn't you go to work? Where is Bella?"

"I want you, Alexandra." He smiled lasciviously. "I've been watching you when you get undressed, and through the curtains when you showered."

Alexandra wanted to scream, but she couldn't. She lay as though in shock, listening to what she didn't want to hear or know. Willie's voice, however, seemed to sound distorted in her ears.

"You should know by now," he continued heavily, "that Jules is not going to marry you. He would have done it long ago if he had wanted to, but he doesn't want to. I want you," he said persuasively, convinced that what he was saying was something that she wanted him to say. "I can give you what Jules doesn't want to give you. I can give you love, give you an apartment, and everything you need. Bella doesn't have to know. She is at work right now. I stayed home to make love to you." He touched her arm, putting his libidinous face very close to her. Alexandra stood up abruptly.

"Who and what in the world," she screamed frantically, "makes you think that I like you, that I am going to accept your dirty proposals, and most of all that I am going to betray my friend Bella when she has been so generous to host me in her house?" Her eyes were gleaming with anger. "Who do you think I am? If you don't have honor with your wife, I do. I could never make love to you, you hear? Never! Guys like you make me sick!"

"Don't tell Bella, please," he begged, looking at her fearfully. "She's not going to believe you if you do."

Alexandra looked at him with pity. "No," she said firmly, "I am not going to tell her, but I am not doing it because of you, but because of her. She doesn't deserve to have the pain that this would give her. You don't deserve Bella, and she doesn't deserve you. Now, if you don't mind," she added, "I need to get dressed, and I don't need you as a witness."

Willie, caught off guard by her reaction, had moved to one corner of the room. His face had a fainthearted grimace. "You are not going to tell Jules, are you? He won't believe you either. He will believe me."

"If I do or don't tell him is something that you don't have to know." Alexandra remarked impatiently. Didn't you hear? Leave!"

Willie turned biting his lips, and strode through the door. Alexandra took five minutes to get dressed and then went out. Teardrops of fury were falling down her face as she walked. Her father had often related to them the story of Diogenes, a philosopher in ancient Greece, who had walked Athens with a lantern in his hands looking in every corner of the city for an honest man, but he found none. Diogenes conclusions were not far from her truth. It was indeed very hard to find in love relations an honest man.

"I can't take it anymore!" Alexandra said to herself as she arrived to Central Park. "I am going back to Mexico."

Somehow the epic had unfolded opposite to her desires. Jules hadn't proposed her to marry him, and the myth of how much men appreciate the women's trophy of virginity was, after all, only a myth. Jules had more interest in her before he made love to her, than after. And then, she had met men like, Ralph, and Willie.

Feeling desolate, she sat on the grass and looked at the pigeons that gathered nearby. Farther away some ducks swam happily, scratching their feathers from time to time, unaware of all suffering. She sighed and raised her eyes; beyond the park, the sky was half covered by lifeless masses of steel. It was amazing to be able to preserve Central Park, this piece of solace and beauty in the middle of a technical and artificial world.

42

"I am going back to Mexico."

Mariana, who was feeding her baby, looked at Alexandra in surprise. "Why?"

Alexandra blinked twice, first gazing towards the window, and then glancing rapidly at her sister. Mariana had a beautiful baby boy now, and things were going great between her and her boyfriend.

"I am tired of all of this farce," Alexandra said after a moment of reflection. Her eyes were fixed on the window. "At the beginning there was the excitement to be here; now that is over. I can't take it anymore. I am not giving up, I just haven't been able to adjust to the hollow mindedness and insensitivity of the life in New York, and to many people who have no sense of decency, and for whom everything is valid. That's all."

"I know what you mean. I don't like that either, but I am happy here, at least for now," Mariana rationalized. "When are you leaving?"

"Tomorrow," Alexandra said, walking towards the door. "I'm quitting work, today." She stopped in her steps, "take care of yourself and the baby, you hear? He is absolutely beautiful."

"I will," her sister said. "Take care of yourself, too, and let me know soon how everything is with the kids down there."

They kissed and she left. All Alexandra needed to do that night was to pack and let Bella know that she was leaving. She turned her head, and waved goodbye to her sister once more.

43

"Child, I am very sorry to hear that you are leaving." Bella said, surprised and sad as her sister had been. "I wish you didn't have to go, that you could stay here with us." As she spoke she came to where Alexandra was standing and held her.

"Are you sure that you don't want to change your mind?" Bella said, almost crying. "If you go," she uttered sorrowfully, "you are not going to see my baby. It's due next month--don't you want to stay at least until then so you can see him?"

"Bella, it's not that. I would like to stay, but I can't." Alexandra said, avoiding Bella's eyes.

"Oh child, I am truly sorry."

If you only knew why, if you only knew, she thought, glancing at Willie. He was sitting on a nearby chair, listening to what was going with alarm.

"All right. If that is what you want, we respect that, but promise me that you'll write."

"I will write," she said briefly, turning her back and staring with disgust at Willie, who was now breathing with relief.

"Have you told Jules that you are going back?" Bella asked.

"No, I haven't, but I am going to stop in New Orleans to see him before I go back to Mexico."

Despite all she still loved him. It was as if she had buried their last encounter and the letters she found in the utmost depths of her heart where the memory couldn't hurt her anymore.

44

New York was behind--the noise, the impersonal superficial life. New Orleans was the same as when she left. The temperature was warm and damp. The sky was blue as it had always been. The flowers were sprightly and fragrant. Alexandra breathed with delight. She was going to see Jules, but had no idea what would be his reaction.

When she stepped into his office unannounced as she had done the last time, Jules looked at her with disbelief. It was 5 p.m. and he was just finishing the day's work. He seemed a little nervous, but only for a fraction of a second.

Alexandra smiled openly and asked, "Are you going to meet Darla?"

Jules glanced at her briefly and continued to open and close his desk drawers as if he were looking for something.

"She moved to Washington D.C.," he said, looking at her for the first time as he threw some papers in the garbage.

"Oh," she responded stupidly, completely astounded.

"I have to take a group of South American students to the French Quarter in the next few minutes," he said, looking at his watch and heading to the door. "Do you want to come?"

"Yes," she replied, still startled as she followed him.

A dozen students were waiting for Jules outside the dorms. Since the moment they perceived Jules approaching, they cheered and greeted him with noted excitement, patting him on the shoulder.

"Hi, how is it going, **cuate**?" one said. The others laughed with that contagious festivity and joviality that characterized Latin American guys.

"Are you ready, **muchachos**? Jules asked.

"**Si, cuate**, we are!"

Then they all stacked together inside the two cars and headed towards downtown New Orleans, joking and laughing.

Bourbon Street, was maddeningly lively. Hordes of people walked along the street sightseeing or going in and out of the bars and the restaurants. For the exchange students from Latin America, this street was a blast, something that in their native countries was forbidden. In Latin America there were no places where topless women and transvestites danced over counter tops accepting men and women favors, nor a center stage where people performed naked live sex.

Alexandra felt a little shy walking among them and witnessing the awakening of their sensuous desires before the obscenities that they had never seen so openly. This world of entertainment was one that she did not favor. She walked ahead of them discreetly. Men always glanced at her when she walked. The rich folds of her dress delineated perfectly her undulating body.

"I'm going to the plaza while the students look at the things around here," she said to Jules. "I'll meet you at the Mexican restaurant in about an hour."

Jules assented in silence, understanding perhaps her discomfort and restlessness as Alexandra dashed up the street. For some reason this evening Jules had been more friendly with her. His eyes, when she had glanced at him every so often, had met hers.

Just a year ago she had been there, loving him madly, but all she had received was deception. Jules didn't know, but the airplane that would take her to Mexico was leaving early in the morning. Tonight was their good-bye.

The tour to the French Quarter wasn't over until half past midnight. Jules took everyone back to the school dorms, and then, he took her to his apartment. He no longer lived in Bridge City. He had moved to New Orleans near Loyola University.

She followed him inside the house silently, and when he held her in the dark, she held him back with all the love and passion that she felt for him.

"I love you!" she cried, dazed.

"No!" he screamed, pushing her away from him abruptly and turning the light on. His face was contorted with fury. "I didn't mean to do that. You must be Satan tempting me! I don't love you! Get dressed!" he reached out for her clothes and threw them violently over the bed where a minute ago he had made love to her.

She was quivering, and a blush of shame covered her body. But there was something savage and chilling in his ways.

"I didn't ask you to come." He now reached for his clothes and got dressed. "I am here alone, and you always come to provoke me. I don't want you to love me. I don't love you; don't you understand? I don't know what I have done to deserve this hell!"

Alexandra grabbed her clothes, and stumbled through the bedroom door, destroyed. Her head was numb and her eyes were dry despite the intense desire that she had to cry. She went to one corner of the living room and sat on the floor near the immense window. The roar of distant thunder broke the silence. The sky was silvery, and heavy drops of rain were hitting the ground furiously. It was hot and humid, but she was shivering.

The clouds had gathered with the wind quickly, turning the weather inclement. Hours before it had been a peaceful night.

A tear began to roll down her face. She stood up and went across the room, opened the front door and strode into the rain, raising her arms and breaking into sudden laughter.

"What are you doing? Have you gone crazy?" Jules demanded furiously.

She giggled with eerie laughter.

"Get in!" Jules said, unhinged from the porch. "You are going to wake up the neighbors."

She continued to laugh loudly.

"Why do you always come to cause me trouble?" His face was livid.

She stopped her laughter and looked at him, then, she came one step closer to where he stood.

"No matter what you said to me, you will remember tonight, Jules Cartier," she boasted, looking straight into his eyes. "You will remember my touch and my love." Her eyes were glistening. "You will remember me, because no one will ever touch you or love you like I have. Tonight will haunt you forever. You, who hate me so grandly, won't be able to forget me! Isn't that the funniest thing you ever heard? Ha! ha!"

He came in rage after her. He grabbed her arms and pushed her into the apartment. Alexandra pulled away defiantly. The rain had washed away her tears.

"Don't touch me!" she snapped, her face a mask of pain. She passed him quickly across the room, reached for the phone and dialed a number hastily. Her hands were trembling.

"What are you doing?" he demanded.

"Hello, can you send a taxi to 3000 Fontainebleau. Thanks."

"Where are you going?"

She got her small suitcase and walked towards the window, ignoring him.

"You are the most incomprehensible, intriguing person I ever met," she heard him complaining.

The taxi driver was soon at the door, ringing the bell. She raced to the door past Jules. Suddenly, she turned and glanced at him briefly for the last time before stepping out. A scorching sensation was hurting her inside, bringing to her mouth a bitter flavor.

"I am going home," she said, getting into the taxi.

Through the cab window her eyes met his eyes, austere and hard as always.

BACK TO MEXICO

Poverty in Mexico City abounded. It was in the narrow and dirty streets, in the small homes that were piled close to one another. It was in the transportation, in the pollution, in the rag pickers and beggars sitting and standing at either side of the populated roads. Undeniably Mexico City, compared to the cities she had seen in the United States, was dirty and poor. But the Mexican people didn't hide their laughter, their good humor, their tender feelings or joyful wit. In Mexico, people were simply who they were.

It is certainly a problem, she thought, glancing at the dozens of dispossessed children who were selling gum and newspapers on the streets, not to have enough schools in the country where children can learn and develop their talents. She looked in the distance. Mexico city was rich in history, noble spirits, courage, ideals, and dreams. But, she had to admit it lacked the wealth that she had seen in the Unites States. In Mexico, only a few of the residents had permanent hot water, refrigerators, televisions, telephones, cars, or other material things. Were, lack of sophistication and duplicity intrinsic to poverty, as were frivolity and hypocrisy intrinsic to wealth? Alexandra couldn't help but wondered glancing at the places that were familiar to her, yet distant. She had come to find refuge, but home since her mother's death, had lost its real meaning.

When the taxi left her in front of the house, she raced into the house joyfully. Her brothers and sisters were in the receiving room, lined up with timid smiles, waiting to greet her. They didn't seem very enthusiastic, but she held them and kissed them all the same.

Who would have known that three years and death would change us all, she thought with nostalgia as she kissed them.

46

Her time in the U.S. receded from her memory in the flurry of getting a job and keeping up with her daily tasks. However, a soft pain came during the night, faintly, bringing to Alexandra's heart a dull disenchantment, ghostly shadows, and tears that she wiped violently as they flowed out, no longer able to contain them. No matter how much she wanted to convince herself of the contrary, part of herself, had stayed in New York, where she ran so freely on the Riverside, and also in New Orleans, where her dreams had shattered.

Alexandra left the doctor's office pretending to be calm, but her head spun crazily. She couldn't believe it. When she stopped in New Orleans, she had made love with Jules only once, but the doctor had just told her she was pregnant. She had the sensation of whirling inside a rapid stream that was robbing her of reason, bombarding her brain with a mixture of feelings and sensations.

Alexandra began to run as she always did when she confronted something that disturbed her. The pregnancy marveled her and terrified her just the same. In the whole world, there was no other venture like accepting the challenge of motherhood. It was by far the most adventurous, the most thrilling, the most daring and purifying of all life ventures but it was also the most frightening. It required more responsibility, more care, more selflessness and dedication that she had ever given. It was terrifying to think of the changes she would experience in her body, and almost incomprehensible to realize that a little being was taking shape inside her body, foreign to duplicity and malice.

Single motherhood in Mexico was not going to be easy. Her pregnancy would inspire women's damning looks, as for men it would inspire malicious propositions.

Mexican society was very restrictive and harsh about sexual matters. It was socially expected that women, though not men, abide by strict moral rules. Women who didn't were looked down upon and considered giddy and easy. There were no exceptions. Even her brothers and aunt, as soon as they realized that she was pregnant, treated her disrespectfully, telling her constantly that she was a free soul who had gone to the U.S. with the sole purpose of allowing free run to her immoral passions.

No matter what everybody thought and said. She had made up her mind to go through the pregnancy despite her own concerns. She loved that baby more than anything. In Jules' life, she had become one more on his list, one more who had become impregnated by him, captivated by his body and his lies.

47

"Hi, how are you doing?"

Before Alexandra was the surprised face of Hilda, looking at her as if she had come back from the dead.

"Hi," Hilda said reluctantly. "When did you come back?"

"A month ago. How is everything with you?"

"Well," she said, "I can't complain." She had the door half open and she was dressed in a worn-out robe. She was pale, and nothing remained of the bright, luminous personality that used to be Hilda.

"Can I come in?" Alexandra inquired.

"Yes, yes, I am sorry," Hilda apologized, opening the door. "You surprised me so much that I wasn't thinking right."

"I heard you had a baby girl; may I see her?"

"Sure, she is here. Come in," she said, walking nervously towards the bedroom.

"Wow, how pretty she is! You must be a very proud mother, uh?" Alexandra exclaimed, taking the beautiful child in her arms.

Hilda half smiled, looking at the austere face of her mother who was reading a book, sitting at the edge of the bed near the crib.

"Hi, Mrs. Martinez. How are you today?" Alexandra greeted her politely.

Mrs. Martinez set the book that she had in her hands to one side of the bed, stood up, and left the room. Hilda's mother had always been like that; an unfriendly face in the crowd, and a mouth of few words. By the severity of her countenance, Alexandra assumed that Hilda's mother blamed her in part for her daughter's pregnancy. After all, Hilda had left with her sister to go to the U.S.

"Will you come to visit me sometime?" Alexandra asked Hilda before she left.

"Yes," Hilda answered. But the days went by, and it never happened that way. Work took most of their time, and other duties made it impossible. Those were the most feasible excuses they could find to avoid confronting each other to reminisce over times past when they were younger, lacked subterfuge, and didn't yet know that life could be so harsh.

48

Alexandra's little baby boy started to kick during the night, breaking the sac where he floated.

"It is time for him to come to the world," she said looking at the clock. It was 12 mid-night.

She got dressed, packed the little covers she had ready for the baby in a small sack, and stormed out into the night, looking for a taxi in the nearest avenue. Her job dispensed medical coverage, but when she got to her provider, they couldn't take her--the hospital had no rooms left. They transported her to a subsidiary, a small, dirty, old clinic at the other side of the city, standing up inside an ambulance with six other parturient women who were screaming their heads off while they traveled.

Like cattle, they squeezed together inside the ambulance holding onto a handle bar that ran across the ambulance's roof as the merciless drivers sped crazily on the streets to get quickly to the clinic. Alexandra was too frightened to scream, even though it hurt so badly. Besides, she didn't want to do anything that could transmit to her little baby boy the idea that he was unwanted.

The women that were traveling with her looked and sounded pathetic. Alexandra stared at them, petrified. They moaned, cried, and yelled cursing all saints, and heaven and hell for their present aches. She had submitted herself to Jules. Now, she had to face the consequences of her choice, the pain and all of what was to come with stoicism, solemnity, and love.

49

Alexandra shivered. It was so cold in the room they assigned her. She was naked but could do nothing about it. The clinic had so many women in labor that night, that there were no robes or cover sheets left for her or anybody else to wear. What was about to happen to her she didn't know, but the eight women who lay naked in the same room with her, were wailing pitifully, uttering chilling screams that the baby they were about to have would be their last one.

"Everything is going to be all right," she kept repeating to herself, trying not to think about the incredible pain that was assailing her body.

In this clinic, there was no anesthesia, no heater, no pain-killers, and no special attention. Alexandra was sweating copiously, despite the fact that she was freezing. She didn't remember ever being this cold and having this intense tremor produced by the tension of her body.

"You ladies complain and implore to all the saints in this moment of truth, but you forgot to implore them and to complain when you had sex with your husbands and asked them for a little more!"

This was the nurses' crude remark every time they came into the room checking out each of the patients for any signs of fever and uterus dilation. They looked dreadful in their white gowns, accomplishing what they had to accomplish with precision, but showed no signs of mercy towards the mothers-to-be. They were too much accustomed to the screaming that took place everyday before delivery to have any compassion. The remark was for Alexandra so out of hand and inappropriate.

Twelve hours later she had her little boy. When the time came she felt like fainting from the pain, but now that it was all over, the pain was forgotten. Her baby was extraordinarily beautiful, perfect, and so, incredibly little! His eyes were closed and his feet and hands were exquisitely well formed. She felt a profound relief to see him healthy and complete.

She drew her baby close, almost afraid to touch him. He seemed so tiny and frail. She kissed his forehead with tenderness, as a shower of happiness inundated her soul.

"Little one, sweet little one," she whispered.

On the third floor the women who had already delivered their babies gathered around her bed.

"He doesn't look like you," one said.

"He is so different," another remarked.

"He is so little and dark..."

"Does he look like your husband?"

"Where is your husband?"

Alexandra thought that her life and suffering were hers.

"My husband is on a trip," she answered. "And yes, my baby looks like him. He is from Haiti."

"He is so cute." One said, giggling.

But they didn't have to say with words for her to know what they were really thinking. It was so obvious by their remarks.

50

After her baby was born, things at home weren't easy. While she went to work, her two brothers were hurting her little son. Her little sister gave her the news one evening.

"Look," they said, as they blew the smoke of their cigarettes in her child's face, "the little idiot laughs when we call him ape. Isn't that funny? The poor thing is so ugly!"

The nasty news not only caused her a heated argument with them, but it also left her drained and depressed.

"You are some kind of monsters," she confronted them.

"We don't like him," one of them said, "what part isn't clear for you?"

She looked at them despondently and walked out of their room. It had been a mistake to come back to Mexico from New York. All she wanted was to find a place where she could live in peace with her son, but all she found was some sort of hell. She wiped the tears from her eyes. One of her father's dissertations resounded in her ears: "a friend is far more dangerous than an enemy, because the enemy is already known as such; not so, the 'friend'." It was a judicious statement, but in this case, the ones to be careful of, were her brothers not her friends.

As for her sister Mariana, she had broken with her boyfriend and had come to visit for a few days. She was physically all right, but her character, as it had happened with Hilda when her boyfriend left her, was transformed. Mariana did not portray depression as Hilda did, but she had acquired vulgar gestures. Her beautiful black hair was now dyed red with lighter lines here and there. She dressed immodestly, and her mode of speech was profane. Since she arrived, she did nothing but fight with Alexandra and tell that her child was ugly and monstrous. She also partied everyday and slept in until finally, after a few weeks of such a frantic life, she departed again to the United States, taking with her most of Alexandra's clothes and other belongings while Alexandra was at work.

Alexandra looked into the empty closet and at herself in the mirror. Her vibrancy from old days had faded away to leave only a shade of grief. Her family as long as she could remember, hadn't been a family of love, but a family of rancor and hate. Alexandra's grandfather hated his son--Alexandra's father. He considered him the family's disgrace, and her dad's only brother also detested him, because he had married the woman they both loved. No one in the extended family talked to them—his children. All of them were despised. They had done nothing improper, but their family and people they knew treated them as if they had. It was as if their father's drinking had totally depersonalized them and tagged them socially as "children of an alcoholic." They had been a "very peculiar family," Alexandra could say, and the labels were more than dreary--they caused a lot of harm, she knew that well.

51

A few days before Christmas, she came face to face with Jules. The memory of their last time together in New Orleans still hurt her. However, he didn't seem to remember. He was waiting with insolent impudence at her aunt's door to meet his baby.

"Come to see me tonight," he said, interrupting her recollections. "I am staying at the Hilton Hotel in room 205. Bring the baby."

"What for?" she asked.

"So we can spend the night together." He held her hand as he said it.

Alexandra felt like she'd been slapped in her face. "Do you think that I am really that easy?" She was breathing hard out of humiliation. "That you can take me and leave me anytime you want?"

"You have a kid from me," he said, as though bragging. "What do you have to loose?"

She looked at him a little sick. "If I were a man," she fired, "I would break your neck."

Jules looked away as though to hide his momentary confusion, then he said.

"I have to go."

"Go." Alexandra said, and Jules left.

52

After her grandmother died, there were always quarrels. No matter who started them, the eighty-year old aunt that had taken over the affairs of the house, chastised Alexandra as the instigator.

"You have a big ego, Alexandra. You think you are worth something, but you are worth nothing. Nothing, you hear? Your fall will be great, just wait and see." Her aunt was reproving when she addressed her. She was always sitting by the entrance of the house, dressed in black, her wrinkled face hidden under the frame of the black shawl that she wrapped around her head. Looking at her always gave Alexandra the creeps. Since she was a child, Alexandra remembered, that aunt had held great dislike for her.

"Rejoice your April and May while they last--your August soon will come!" The voice of her aunt sounded in Alexandra's head loud and clear, cursing her life with malediction and omens of affliction.

She held her son Franco and went up to the roof not to hear her anymore. The earth lay beneath her feet, benign and plentiful, rich in beauty and wonder, but the world, and people she knew were frequently complicated and ugly. Love and peace seemed remote and detached. She stared in the distance; on the horizon the sky had turned gray, as if the sky would be protesting and showing its displeasure for all unkind occurrences. She sat on the floor and caressed her child. To live safely and at peace, she had to get out of there. A pleasant environment was essential, but where was such a phantom place?

"Utah! That's it!" She screamed. "Why didn't I think of that before?"

Utah was a Mormon state. In the early 1800's, Pioneers of The Mormon Church, persecuted, vexed, and killed by intolerant and fanatical mobs, crossed the plains in search of religious freedom. Convinced by decree of their prophet, they founded the prosperous city of Salt Lake when he indicated to the saints that followed him that they had arrived at the chosen place. Warren lives in Utah, she thought, but would he be willing to help me now that many years have passed? Well, she concluded, there is only way to find out.

53

"Hello?" Alexandra heard a feminine voice at the other end of the line.

"Hello," Alexandra said. "May I talk to Warren?"

"One moment, please."

After a minute that seemed an hour, Warren Maxwell was on the line.

"Hello?" he said.

"Warren? This is Alexandra, do you remember me?"

"How are you doing, Alexandra?" he said. "What a surprise!"

"I'm fine, and you?"

"I'm fine," Warren stated, laughing a little. "I got married a few years ago. And you, did you get married?"

"No," she said, embarrassed. "I didn't get married, but I have a little son from Jules. Do you remember Jules?"

"Yes, the one you told me you were going to marry."

"Yes, I remember I told you that. I wanted to marry him, but he didn't want to marry me."

"It's too bad," he said after a moment of silence. "Who would have known that things were going to be like this?"

Alexandra didn't answer. She closed her eyes. Warren Maxwell had come to say goodbye. He had stars in his eyes--his time as a missionary for the Church of Jesus Christ in Mexico had come to an end.

She shook her head, coming back from the past to the present.

"Yes, who could have known that things would turn out this way?" She tried to sound natural.

"I met Alysjo a few years ago, and got married," he revealed. "I have four kids now."

She couldn't talk.

"Alexandra, what do you need?" Warren asked.

"I want to go to Utah. I want to ask you that if I go, if it would be possible to stay in your home until I am able to get a job and a place to live?"

"Of course you can," he said affably. "You will always be welcome in my house."

"What about your wife?" Alexandra inquired apprehensively. "Will it be all right for her?"

"It will be if I say it's all right."

"Are you sure?"

"I'm sure." He laughed with tenderness. "When are you coming?"

"I'm not sure. I need to take care of some things first. But it will be soon. I will call you from the airport to pick me up."

"O.K." he said. "In the meantime, don't worry about my wife--everything will be fine."

"Thank you. I'll see you soon then."

"Bye."

GOING BACK

The immigration laws to enter the United States were difficult and tight. Not everybody who lined up early in the morning at the American Embassy waiting to get a visa was lucky enough to get it. Many came out of the building with a frown of disappointment, their lives definitely changed.

Her heart was shaking. She pressed the passport nervously inside her pocket and looked straight ahead; there were only two more people in front of her, and then it would be her turn to be interrogated by the immigration officer. She needed to appear calm and secure, when her turn came, even though inside she was a wreck. She had waited patiently for more than three hours. She breathed deeply.

"Next!" the American man behind the counter demanded arrogantly.

Alexandra advanced smiling.

"Good morning!" she said.

"Your passport?" the man at the counter asked coldly.

She took out the passport from her pocket and handed it to him nervously.

The man quickly turned the pages of the passport. "Where are you going?" he asked with hostility.

"I am going to Utah to visit some friends," she replied, smiling.

"Humm," he muttered, looking at her with disdain. "Who is this in the photo?"

"That's my son," she answered politely.

His cold eyes examined the picture for a few seconds in silence.

"Sorry, I can't give you a visa." He scribbled something in the passport and handed it back to her.

"Why not?" she inquired.

"I just can't, that's all," he replied. "Next."

Alexandra bit her lips as she blushed with humiliation, took her passport, and walked away distressed. The man had denied her the visa, but his denial was not going to end her plans. She was determined to go back to the United States.

As she came out of the building, the first drops of rain had begun to fall as distant lightning cut the sky in half. She sped up her pace, walking for the next two blocks until she came to a sudden halt in front of the Telephone Company building. Without hesitation, she went through the revolving door.

"I need to place a long distance call to Canada and pay for the call here." Alexandra told the receptionist politely. "This is the telephone number. I need to speak to Mr. Braulio Perez."

"Please step in booth number 4," the receptionist said.

"Thanks," she said.

When the operator signaled, Alexandra took the phone inside the booth with a shaky hand.

"Hello?"

"Braulio, is that you?"

"Yes, who is this?"

"This is Alexandra. How are you doing?"

"Alexandra, how come this miracle?"

"Well, what can I say? I have no justification for not calling you before, I must say, but now I need you."

There was a silence at the end of the line, then, Braulio said, "What can I do for you?"

"Well, I want to go to the United States, but I was unable to get the visa. I was wondering if I could give your address as a referral, fly to Canada, and enter the United States through the Canadian border?"

"There wouldn't be any problem with that," Braulio responded promptly. Alexandra could see him at the other end of the line, very businesslike, pacing from one side of the room to the other while he talked. "You are welcome to stay with us for as many days as you want, then go to the United States from here. My wife and I have been inviting you to come for so long. This is a nice country. You'll love it!"

"Thank you, Braulio, I appreciate that. I will accept your invitation and stay with you for a few days, but I want to get to my destination as soon as possible."

"I understand. Time is money, as the gringos say."

"I have already wasted a lot of time going back and forth between Mexico and the United States."

"Why is that?"

"Problems. Everywhere I go things come up."

"That happens to everyone. You just have to be patient. When shall we expect you?"

"As soon as I get another passport for me and my son." She paused. "We don't need a visa to get into Canada, do we?"

"No, there is no visa from Mexico to Canada. Your passport would suffice."

"That's what I thought, but I wasn't absolutely sure. I'm glad we don't have to meet that requirement. This makes things easier. How's work and everything?"

"Absolutely wonderful. We love it up here. I don't regret a bit to have asked at work for my transfer. We are doing great. My wife loves it despite the bitter cold."

"I'm glad for you, Braulio. It's good to hear that you are fine, that you guys are well."

"It was about time, after all the adjustments we've been through."

"I think so," Alexandra said briefly. Braulio and Sally had had difficulties and had been many times on the brink of getting a divorce. "I will be there in about a week," Alexandra changed the subject subtly. "I will call you from the airport if I need you, and if I don't, I'll see you at your house."

"O.K, then. It's all set. Make sure you come, you hear? We will be looking forward to seeing you soon."

"You will. Thanks a million! I'll never forget this favor."

"We are forever friends, don't you remember?"

"Yes, I do, thanks."

"Bye."

She hung up, satisfied. She had problems, but she was lucky to have good friends, people that would come to her aid and listen to her. For a moment, when she was at the American Embassy, she had felt without options, forced to live in the midst of hate. But fortunately she had thought of Braulio, her longtime, friend.

Peace was all she was seeking, and a life of her own with her child.

"Hi, my little darling. Guess what? We are going to Canada." Alexandra told her little son, bouncing him in the air. "From there, we will go to Utah. We will be flying in the biggest airplane. You'll see."

"Can we see the clouds from the airplane, mommy?"

"Yes, we can. It will be a marvelous view! You'll love it. Isn't it exciting?"

"Yeah! I want to go on an airplane."

"Pretty soon, my darling. I just need to get another passport and we will be all set to go."

She laughed with hope. The future looked rosy. Nothing could be more important than what she could do for her son and for her, even if that involved going to another country without a legal visa again.

55

Flying was glorious. The earth looked magnificent from the sky. Their luggage was just a few clothes, but Alexandra's heart was replete with courage and dreams. Her little Franco was sitting on her lap, looking at the clouds with a smile. For his happiness she would attempt anything.

Tenochtitlan was behind--the city of the sun, her childhood years buried in disenchantment in the dying horizon. Alexandra wiped her tears and gazed forward. The speed of the mechanical bird was incredible. They crossed two countries in 6 hours and were finally flying over their destination: Toronto, Canada.

The landing was celebrated, as it always was when she had flown, with gabble and applause of the passengers who were brought to safety by the skills of the well train pilots. In life there were so few occasions like this, when among people there weren't barriers but a common feeling uniting them all. Her blood was pumping.

She took Franco's little hand and followed the crowd to customs. She extended her passport to the Canadian official with a secure hand. The officer was very cordial. As he reviewed the papers, Alexandra hid her dread and looked at him in the eye with confidence.

"Are you on vacation?" the officer asked her amiably.

"Yes, I am. I've been told this place is wonderful. I have always had the desire to come."

The Canadian officer smiled, pleased. "It sure is. Well, it's home for us." He smile as he stamped the visa on the passport, then handed it back to her. "Welcome to Canada. Follow that sign to get your luggage."

"Thank you." Alexandra said politely. She wanted to run, to run without stopping just for the feeling of happiness.

Alexandra and Franco got their luggage, then a taxi to Braulio's house.

The city of Toronto was a delight. At this time of the year, it was covered with snow, but it was extraordinarily clean and beautiful. A big thermometer on a high tower read:-26 F degrees.

"Brrr," she said, holding Franco. "It's cold, don't you think?"

"Where are we going now, mommy?" Franco asked. His eyes were wide open, staring out the car window in wonder.

"We are going to Braulio's house. They will like you very much. They are good friends."

"Look at those geese!" Franco exclaimed.

She looked through the car window and saw them. They were flying amazingly low, moving their undulant wings rhythmically. It was an absolutely stupendous scene. She was ecstatic. Life was beautiful, offering them the opportunity to witness all those wonderful things.

"Wow! They are gorgeous," she said.

"Look. There, at the lake!" Franco screamed, pointing with his index finger.

The lake looked like a silvery mirror in which some icebergs floated, resembling huge blocks of marble tarnished by the sun with a patch of gold.

"Wow!" She said. "It looks like heaven on earth, don't you think so?"

"Yeah! I like it here, mommy."

"I do too, my sweet."

Kisses and hugs was their welcome. Braulio and his wife had been married for a few years, had no children, and despite their troubles, were still madly in love.

"Come in, come in--so long without seeing you," Sally said. It's good to have you here, eh? So, this is your little Franco."

"Yes! This is he."

"He is big and handsome. Hi, Franco. Come give me a hug. How old are you?" Sally said.

"Three."

They chatted for an hour, went out for dinner to a fancy restaurant, then, back to Braulio's home, they went to bed.

It would have been nice to stay in Canada; the place was lovely. Canada seemed more peaceful than the United States, and the people, more dignified and kind. It was strange, but history set the mood of the peoples, their heritage, culture and idiosyncrasies. Mexico, in that respect, had no parallel. Alexandra thought, despite the poverty, it was a land of warriors.

56

"We are leaving tomorrow, Braulio," Alexandra said that Sunday morning. Two and a half weeks had passed since they arrived. Braulio was behind her on the kitchen table having breakfast.

"Are you sure you don't want to stay a few more days? It has been fun having you."

"I would, but I can't. I need to get a job as soon as possible. Franco needs to enroll in school."

Braulio's face was very serious. "Don't take me wrong, Alexandra, but if you go to the U.S. and find difficulties, stay. Don't go back to Mexico. Moving every time you have trouble will get you nowhere."

"You are right. I have thought of that too." She bit her lips, worried and embarrassed that Braulio knew her so well.

"Please don't take this as a reprimand. I wouldn't interfere, but I love you, and I want you to be happy."

"I'm not upset. I don't take you wrong, Braulio. I appreciate what you told me, and will remember your advice when I feel discouraged."

"Well, I hope so." He arranged his tie. "What time are you leaving?"

"We are leaving early in the morning. We are going by bus to Chicago, and there I will take a plane to Utah."

"Do you have everything ready?" He looked at her with concern. "Have you figured out what to say?"

"Pretty much. When they check my passport, I am going to say I am on my way back to Mexico. That way they won't suspect I am going to stay in the United States."

"I wish you luck. Drop us a note when you get to Utah so we know everything went according to plan."

"I will. Thanks for letting me come up here. I couldn't have made it to the States without your help. I'm deeply grateful. Sally is wonderful."

"Yes, she is a nice girl."

"As soon as she comes back from work, I'll let her know that we are leaving tomorrow."

"She'll be sorry. She loves your little Franco. I love Franco." He turned and held the young boy. "We love you. You are a nice and handsome boy, do you know that?"

"I love Sally and you, too," Franco said.

Alexandra smiled. Everything was set; they were again ready to undertake another trip.

57

Alexandra and Franco had no problems crossing the border. For the U.S. immigration, they were on their way to Mexico. The United States officer extended them the two weeks visa without delay.

It had been a risky but smart and ingenious try, and she had succeeded. Two weeks was all she needed to disappear—first in Detroit, then, in Chicago.

As soon as they crossed the Canadian border, the life pace increased. There were more people on the streets, more cars, more buildings lined together, narrower and dirtier streets. The feeling she had inside was exhilarating, hard to control. They were finally in the U.S.

"Warren?" she said on the phone.

"Yes?"

"This is Alexandra. I am coming into Salt Lake City at 6 p.m. on Delta."

"We'll be there to get you."

"Thanks."

"See you later."

What an adventure she thought, breathing with relief after she hung up. She had taken two months after their last conversation preparing everything to go across the border. She held her little son close to her heart as they left the O'Hare airport and Chicago behind.

The airplane landed in Salt Lake City on time. Alexandra held her little son's hand and they rushed through the long halls to get their small suitcase. Then, with anxious eyes, she started to look for the familiar face of Warren in the crowd.

He was taller than most, so it wasn't very hard to find him. Holding her little son's hand, she got close to where he was. The surprised eyes of Warren met hers as a big smile crossed his face.

"There you are, sweet lady!" Warren said as Alexandra and Franco stopped in front of him.

Standing by Warren were his pregnant wife and his four children, two girls and two boys.

"Hi!" Alexandra turned to them and hugged them one by one. "This is my son."

"Look at the little fellow!" Warren said happily, taking her son in his arms. You are a handsome little boy, did you know that?"

Franco, who wasn't accustomed to receiving any signs of affection from men, smiled with brightest eyes. The shine in her little son's eyes never ceased to amaze Alexandra, he had the most beautiful eyes that a little boy could ever have. For him, this was a completely new world, too many things to handle all at once, but Franco appeared to be accepting them with stoic courage.

As they chatted, Alysjo, Warren's wife, was standing in silence, looking at them with misgivings. Her smile was faked, and by her looks Alexandra knew that she was displeased with their presence.

"We have the truck in the parking lot. Let's go," Warren said.

He carried their luggage, and they followed him.

"This is our car," Warren said, pointing at a big truck that he used to conduct his business of landscaping and trimming trees. "Come on, Alexandra, get in. Don't be afraid. We'll make you feel at home." He lifted Franco in his arms and sat him inside the truck.

Springville, where they lived, was about 50 minutes from Salt Lake, but the trip seemed shorter with the excitement. Warren didn't cease talking and the kids were laughing and singing.

Alexandra was nervous. She needed to get a job fast and move from their house as soon as possible. She didn't want to prolong their stay and cause trouble. Warren's wife wasn't pretty. She seemed a little older than he was and didn't put any effort into attracting her husband by her looks.

"Here it is--this is our home," Warren said, getting out of the truck and helping everyone else to get out. "Alysjo, show

Alexandra and Franco their bedroom. I'm going to mom's house to tell her we made it. I'll be right back."

Alysjo nodded silently.

"This way," she said, as she walked inside the house followed by her children, Alexandra, and Franco.

Their house was nice but very untidy. Alexandra bit her lip. The mess was so obvious that it couldn't be disguised; the dirt was everywhere.

"Sit down," Alysjo invited her.

Alexandra sat on the sofa and looked around. The living room was grand. It had a precious fire in the corner, and the walls were made of expensive wood. A green carpet covered the floor, some rifles hung from the wall, and clothes, toys, and unclean dishes were scattered on the sofas, television, and on the floor, taking away the enchantment of what otherwise would be a beautiful residence.

Franco had started to play on the floor with the boys and they were laughing.

"I'll show you to your bedroom," Alysjo said, taking her to the north part of the house.

It was a nice bedroom, but like the rest of the house, everything in it was in a jumble.

"These are some clean sheets," Alysjo said to Alexandra, handing her a pair of clean sheets and pillowcases.

"Warren and I sleep here," she indicated, pointing at the master bedroom that was on the right. "My daughters sleep here and the boys here."

Alexandra followed her in silence.

"What are you two doing?" Warren asked with his familiar good humor, getting between them as he spoke. "Are you two getting along?" He had a big smile on his face.

"Oh, shut up," Alysjo said. "You have no business here."

But Warren stayed right there, by the door, staring at Alexandra. Alexandra purposely avoided his eyes, not wanting to read his thoughts.

"Thank you, Alysjo," Alexandra said. "I will take care of the bed."

"O.K." Alysjo said, leaving the room. "Call me if you need anything," Alexandra began to make the bed under the silent scrutiny of Warren, who apparently had no intentions of leaving the post he had taken by the door.

"It's good to see you, girl," he said when Alysjo was gone.

"It's good to see you, too, mister." Alexandra smiled, glancing quickly at him. "You have a lovely family."

"Well," he said, looking around as he raised his shoulders, "this is not the best, but we want you to feel at home."

"I feel at home," she said, looking away.

"Mommy, mommy, where are you?" Franco called, coming into the room looking for her, "come and see the game that they have. It's fabulous!"

She held him in her arms and, carrying him, she walked towards the living room followed by Warren.

"Come, little fellow, you are all right," Warren said, taking Franco from Alexandra's arms kissing the child and bouncing him in the air.

Despite the dirt, it was nice to be in the midst of a real Mormon family. Mormon customs were different from those of other churches. Church was not only a Sunday affair. God played an active part in the every-day lives of its members.

"All right kids, come on over to offer a word of prayer." Warren directed them before bedtime. "Hurry! Get here you flock."

At the sound of his voice, Alysjo and his kids stopped what they were doing to get together to pray. Once reunited in the living room, they knelt in reverence.

"Loving and kind Heavenly Father..." Warren began.

Before closing her eyes, Alexandra observed them for a second. It was good to be with them, feeling that warmth inside her heart as a testimony of the presence of the Lord in that very room.

58

Alysjo was not lazy. She tried cleaning the house, but for some reason, despite her work and effort, by the time Warren came back from work every night, dinner was never ready, and the house looked as if a cyclone had passed through it, moving everything out of place.

"Oh, Alysjo," he whined, upset that evening, "what do you do all day long that you are never able to have dinner ready and a clean house?"

Alexandra, who was helping Alysjo sweep the kitchen floor, lowered her eyes, wishing Warren hadn't made her part of their little problems. It wasn't pleasant to hear them quarreling knowing the imposition she had brought upon them by lodging in their house so unexpectedly. Discretely, she left the kitchen, praying that she could move soon.

Two weeks later, she got a job. It wasn't a great job, but living in a small town like this one, it was the best she could get. A month and a half later, she rented an apartment close to work and the school Franco would be attending.

"Thanks for everything," Alexandra said appreciatively, when Alysjo and Warren brought them to their new apartment.

"We are glad we could help," Warren answered. "Call us if you need anything."

"We will," Alexandra said nervously. "Thank you."

59

It was only a few days after they moved that Warren came to visit. He had that blaze in his eyes and he was smiling.

"Hi," he greeted. "May I come in?"

"Hi," Alexandra said shyly, opening the door to let him in.

"How are you guys doing? Is everything all right?" His voice was at once happy and anxious.

"We're fine." Alexandra said as her little boy came running out of the bedroom.

"Hi," Franco said as he came to a halt, looking at Warren in surprise.

"How are you, little fellow?" Warren said fraternally, grabbing him in one step and lifting him in the air.

"Fine," Franco said, smiling happily.

"Would you like to sit down?" Alexandra offered.

"Nope," Warren said firmly. "I better keep going, I just came to check if you were all right."

"We are."

Warren gazed at her inquisitively for a moment.

"Is there anything I can help you with?"

"No, Warren. Thanks." Alexandra answered, as she glanced distractedly through the window.

"Well, then..." He advanced as though he had changed his mind to leave and he sat on the sofa with her child still in his arms, staring at her with delight. Then he asked, "How do you do it, working and still keeping this place so clean?"

She stared at him for a second, then, lowered her eyes. He made her nervous, because his eyes couldn't hide the attraction that he felt for her. He told her so in every look that he gave her, in every move he made.

"Well, I am going," he said. "I'll see you tomorrow." He kissed Franco and let him off his arms as he stood up.

Her son smiled, pleased, and hand in hand he walked his new friend to the door.

"Bye, Warren," Franco said.

"Bye," Alexandra waved from the kitchen.

60

From then on Warren came to visit them every day. He stopped for an hour in the evening on his way back home, sat on the sofa, played with Franco, then, left.

"I just came to check on you," he always said.

It was terribly disturbing to have him there, to act naturally, pretending not to notice the ardent look in his eyes.

"Let's go for a ride," Warren asked her one Saturday afternoon.

Unlike other days, he stood by the door with a grave expression on his face.

"Well," she said thoughtfully, surprised by the seriousness on his face, "let me ask Gloria if she can take care of Franco while we go."

Warren nodded.

Something must be wrong, Alexandra thought as she stepped into the bedroom where she found Gloria reading. Gloria had come from Mexico to live with her three months ago. They met when she was pregnant with Franco.

"Gloria, Warren is here. I am going to go with him for a ride. Can you take care of Franco? I won't take long, just a few minutes."

"O.K." Gloria nodded. "What's wrong?"

"I'm not sure. I'll be back."

Alexandra stepped into the other bedroom where Franco was playing with his train track.

"Sweetheart, I am going with Warren for a few minutes, I will be back."

"O.K., mommy," Franco answered as he continued playing.

She followed Warren to the truck. "Where are we going?" she inquired.

"We are going for a short ride around the canyon. Is that okay with you?"

"Yes, it is." She smiled. He was acting so enigmatic.

Warren took the Provo canyon road and drove in silence for a few minutes, glancing at her once in a while.

"Come," he said, parking at one side of the road and helping her out. He went rapidly through the bushes and down between the stones to where the stream of water ran. There he stopped. She felt a tremor. Warren's eyes were fixed on hers, silently telling her all those unspoken things that they had felt for each other for so long. She had been mistaken to reject him when he asked her to marry him, but that had happened so long ago. Now everything had changed. She looked away. The sound of the river was clear and distinct, and it smelled like spring. The trees were full of blossoms. The wind drifted softly down the canyon, cool, and clean.

Warren held her in his arms.

"I love you! I have always loved you," he moaned, no longer able to contain the tension building in himself.

Alexandra looked at him. He was tall and distinguished, masculine and attractive. His eyes were as blue as the sky, and his hair silky and black, slightly disarranged over his forehead.

"I love you!" he repeated, as he looked into her eyes. His immense love was coming to his voice from his soul, real and impetuous, deep and true.

"I love you, too," she said shyly, overtaken by his virile poise and the tone of his voice.

"Oh darling..." he whispered, kissing her with devotion.

Alexandra closed her eyes. It would be nice to stay in his arms and erase the world, she thought. He had all of what she ever wanted in a man. When he came to visit her, there was no doubt. His presence filled the room and her heart.

"What about Alysjo?" She asked, suffocated by his delicious kisses as she pushed him away. "We can't do this to her. She is having your baby soon!"

"I know," Warren said. His face was flushed. "I shouldn't have kissed you, I know, but every time I see you I want to hold you." He looked into the distance, then, continued, "I married her, but I love you. I loved you since I met you. I can divorce her. You know that."

Alexandra looked at him somberly. For a moment his presence had eclipsed the reality. She turned her back on him and walked slowly towards the truck. She was, like him, at the verge of tears. Of all the men she had met, Warren had been the only one who really loved her, the only one who had proposed something clean, and the one she had refused in pursuit of Jules.

Warren followed her in silence to the car, then, drove her back home. There was still that grave expression on his face, a desperate intensity in all his moves and in his eyes.

She had to go away. Neither of them could control the profound attraction, and the repressed feelings. There was no other way to avoid him. His eyes had an irreversible desire, an inevitable love that couldn't change for the sake of duty.

When they got to her apartment complex, Alexandra jumped out of the truck in a hurry.

"Alexandra," Warren called, "I can't stop coming to see you."

She turned and looked at him for a second, then, she ran upstairs, scared. Warren was not going to stop coming to her place, and it was too dangerous for her to take the risk of staying.

Surprised, Gloria raised her eyes from the book that she was reading as Alexandra ran into the room.

"What happened?" Gloria asked apprehensively. "You look like you've seen a ghost."

Alexandra sat down in dismay.

"It's Warren, isn't it?" Gloria asked. "Did he finally confess that he is crazy about you?"

"Yes," Alexandra confirmed, almost breathless.

"It's not your fault. Sooner or later this would have happened. He can't hide it."

Alexandra glanced at her friend in silence. They became friends when they worked the night shift together at the Hilton Hotel in Mexico City. Alexandra was pregnant then, and Gloria had been married at that time to a guy who abused her brutally. He was ill mannered and conceited—the "macho" type. And for that reason she decided to abandon him. She did so one day when he went to work, after he had savagely beaten her, describing to her the numerous ways he made love to other women. Gloria had lost track of Alexandra when she came the U.S., but Gloria, frightened by the thought that her husband could find her, sought Alexandra's whereabouts, traveled to the border, paid a "coyote" a few hundred pesos to take her across the border safely in the trunk of a car, and came to Utah.

"What are you going to do?" Gloria asked.

"Leave!" Alexandra answered emphatically. "Go as far away as possible from here." She paused to catch her breath. The air was suffocating. She stood up and walked about the room nervously, followed by the attentive eyes of her friend. "Warren helped me when I needed it. I don't want to pay him back by destroying his family and causing him problems. I don't want to be involved in adultery, either." Alexandra seemed to be saying this more to herself than to Gloria.

"Alexandra," Gloria said, "I'll go with you wherever you go."

"My sister Mariana lives in New Orleans. I am going to call her and ask her if we can go there." Her voice was low and apprehensive.

"Whatever you want," Gloria said again.

"Where are we going, mommy?" Franco asked, entering the bedroom suddenly.

"To New Orleans."

"Why? Why do we have to leave?"

"My sister is there; we are going to live with her."

61

On Monday evening, as she feared, Warren came. Franco opened the door.

"Mommy, Warren is here!"

Alexandra, who was reading in the bedroom, shuddered, set the book on the bed, and came out. Warren had Franco in his arms, bouncing him up and down as always. When he saw her, he blushed and let go of Franco.

"How are you, beautiful?"

She had to laugh. He had such a delicious, playful way of making everything all right. Then, she diverted her eyes. Warren's eyes were pleading, adoring, caressing, and apologizing. She could have cuddled in his chest.

"Warren," she said, catching her breath, "we are going to move."

"Where?" he asked, perplexed.

"To New Orleans."

A dark frown replaced his enthusiastic smile. "You can't..!"

"Warren, we are."

He was speechless, pacing nervously around the room. "Why? Why are you doing this?" he asked, crazed. His blue eyes seemed to have darkened.

"Because I don't want to take your family away from you, that's why. I don't think I want to hurt you this way."

He was kissing her with his eyes as he advanced slowly towards Franco, who lay on the floor playing, and grabbed him again in his arms.

"I love you, little fellow." He said as he sat down on the rocking chair with Franco on his lap.

Alexandra bit her lips helplessly.

"How awful is all of this," Gloria said in Spanish as she came into the living room.

"When are you guys leaving?" Warren asked, after Gloria left the room.

"When, Franco finishes school in three weeks."

"I don't want to go, but mommy does," Franco interrupted.

Warren patted Franco's back with affection, and after a while, he let go of him. Despite the indisputable efforts to maintain his serenity, Warren looked as if something had hit him. Suddenly he stood up and came towards her, grabbing her by the shoulders.

"Call us if you need anything, if things go wrong, if you need our help again." He searched for her eyes that were avoiding his. "Promise me that you'll do that."

"I promise," she said.

Without saying more, he released her from his touch, crossed the room quickly, and stormed out the door.

"Stay," Warren had asked her, but there she was packing up again, running away once more from shattered dreams in search of peace.

IN NEW ORLEANS

In the city of New Orleans, her sister lived at the end of St. Charles Street. She had moved from New York to New Orleans a couple of years ago into this duplex. She occupied the upstairs with her son, Ronaldo, their eldest brother, and with Adela, the oldest of their little sisters. Life was treating all well, they had good jobs, and this time Mariana had a very handsome boyfriend. Despite the favors, Mariana's moods hadn't changed. She was happy to see Alexandra, but continued with the attitude of dislike towards Franco.

Alexandra loved New Orleans. The green of the land was fantastic. She didn't miss a chance to take her little boy to the Zoo, the parks, the riverbank, and finally when they had exhausted almost everything, she took him to meet his father.

They dressed up, caught the bus, and when they were a few steps away from Jules' house, her nervousness could hardly let her breath. Four years had passed since the last time she had seen him in front of her aunt's house in Mexico, and here she was bringing her child to meet his dad for the first time. With a trembling heart, she knocked at his door.

"Hi!" she said, smiling, slightly shy when Jules opened the door halfway.

But what she saw made her rising hopes vanish. Jules' face depicted the relentless austerity and cold demeanor he had always assumed in her presence.

"I'm busy," he said dryly, closing the door a little bit more.

Alexandra bit her lips in pain and humiliation. She blushed and breathed deeply. Before she could say anything, Jules had closed the door. Alexandra looked at her son, who stood in one corner of the porch waiting to meet his dad. The joy in his eyes had turned to sadness, and in an instant, her pain turned to fury.

"Pig! Beast! Open the door!" she screamed as she hit and kicked the door again and again. "Why do you do this to your son? Open the door you pig, merciless inhuman beast!"

But she couldn't continue. Tears had blinded her eyes and quenched her voice in convulsive sobs.

"Don't cry, mommy, don't cry, please," her little son said with anguish, holding her with his tender arms as he started to cry.

"I am sorry, my little darling, I am so sorry. I didn't mean to scare you. I won't cry anymore. Mommy loves you. Your mommy loves you. Let's go."

She wiped her tears, held her little boy in her arms, and began to walk away. Her feet felt as if they were made of lead. That Jules could be so cruel with his little son was beyond her reasoning. It had been worse than receiving a thousand blows. But it was obvious that he was in his house with someone, perhaps another lover.

Carrying with her the weight of her sadness, she took her son to the zoo as she tried to erase from her son's mind the horrid memory. Seeing the animals was a lot of fun, especially the six chimpanzees that splashed water, spit, and threw banana peels over the viewers who were provoking them by imitating their noises. It was good to hear her son's laughter looking at the chimpanzees and later, when they caught the little train that went around the park.

"Let's run after the ducks, mommy," Franco said.

Alexandra held her son's hand and began to run. The ducks that had ducked at the edge of the pond scattered at once in all directions.

63

Alexandra woke up early, took a shower, wore a red dress with navy blue flowers, navy blue high-heels, combed her hair, and when she was ready, stepped into the street. The streetcar stop was on the corner. She boarded the train almost immediately. At this time of the morning it was overcrowded. She had no specific destination but she was determined to get a job. Suddenly, she noticed a hospital a block away from the stop sign. Excusing herself among the people she rushed to get off.

"Hi," Alexandra said, walking into the Personnel office with a glowing smile. "Can I have an application?"

"Sure," the receptionist said handing her a clipboard with an application pinned on it. "Are you applying for the switchboard operator position?"

"Yes," she answered with a smile, not knowing a position was open.

"Good," said the receptionist. "We need someone right away."

When she finished filling out the application, Alexandra handed it back and was asked to wait.

"Alexandra?" A well-dressed man who had her application in his hands called.

She stood up, smiling.

"Over here, please. After you," the man said, stepping aside to let her go into his office.

"Well, well, well," he said, sitting down, looking at her application with sincere interest. "Are you from New York?"

"Yes." Alexandra smiled.

"Hmm," he murmured, taking one hand to his chin. "You have quite a bit of experience in this kind of job, I see."

"Yes, I do." Alexandra replied firmly. "I have worked in several hotels in New York as an operator and as a front desk clerk."

"What brought you to New Orleans?"

"I like New Orleans," she said sincerely. "This is a lovely place--New York is too crowded."

"You bet," he said. "If we hire you, when can you start?"

"Immediately."

"Well..." the man seemed to reflect. "Today is Friday. Be here on Monday morning at 8 o'clock, I will personally take you to meet your supervisor."

"Thank you very much," she said happily. "I'll be here at 8 o'clock."

"All right Alexandra." He smiled. "Nice to meet you. My name is Glen George."

"Nice to meet you, too."

She walked out, elated. It had been simple, a job at the first try.

64

She had just been working for a few days when Gloria told her "You have to take your child away from here."

They had been sitting on the porch, keeping an eye on Franco and Sean, who played on the sidewalk with their skateboards a few yards away from them.

Alexandra looked at Gloria suspiciously.

"It took me a while to make this decision, but I don't have the heart to keep it from you any longer," she said, utterly nervous. "When you are not here, your sister treats your little boy very badly. I feel sorry for him."

"What does she do?" Alexandra asked her friend, turning pale.

"She hits him and talks to him very harshly, but that's not all. When someone comes to visit and sees him, she tells them that he is not your real son, but an adopted son."

Alexandra felt exhausted all of a sudden. When would the confrontations end? She thought. A deep rage boiled inside her.

She stood up without thinking any further and went to look for her sister. "You don't have the right to hit my son," she scolded "It is very cruel of you to do something like that."

"I don't like him, and you know it. You are in my house. If you don't like the way I am or how I treat your son, move." She said with her habitual coldness.

"I will," Alexandra said, "but first, let me make one thing clear. My son is not adopted. He is mine! You don't have the right to spread news that he is, nor you have the right to hit him. If you have any frustrations, vent them on someone else, and not, on an innocent child who does you no harm."

"Yes, he harms us. He gives us a bad reputation; besides, I don't want him to grow up near my son, otherwise my son won't have any friends. Nobody wants to be friends with someone who has a black in the family," Mariana snapped.

"You are as revolting as everybody else who thinks like you do!" Alexandra yelled, infuriated. "I am going to move, not because it is your desire to have my son away from your son, or to restore your lost reputation. I am going to move, because I can't stand living with someone as hateful as you."

"Whatever." her sister said, yawning with indifference. "But if you move, do it fast. I don't want your monster here anymore. He is so ugly." She turned her back and walked away, ending the discussion.

Trembling, Alexandra sat down, at the verge of tears. Her sister's cruelty was too inhuman to be real.

65

"What happened?" Gloria asked.

Alexandra was still sitting by the window when Gloria came back in.

"We are going to move," Alexandra answered. "We need to find an apartment as soon as possible."

"All right." Gloria said. She was smart enough to know what went on. "Tomorrow is Saturday. We can go around to look for one."

Alexandra assented in silence. After a while she said, "Mariana is absolutely disgusting. She doesn't care about anybody but herself. It's inconceivable!"

"I told you so." Gloria said with a frown of worry. "I am sorry I told you, but I had to. I feel so sorry for Franco when she treats him badly."

Alexandra said nothing else. She stood up and went to the backyard to look for Franco. It was late in the evening, almost time for bed.

"Nothing is fair!" Alexandra screamed that night in her dreams, looking at herself and her little son in the midst of a strange plaza. They were bombarded by the rejection and scorn of a multitude that yelled louder and louder, "We don't want you...! Get Out!"

66

It had been a dream, but had she dreamed? When Alexandra opened her eyes, thick drops of sweat were rolling down her body. Everything was wet, clothes and covers, as if an immense bucket of water had fallen over her. For a moment she sat at the edge of the bed and looked slowly around the room. It had no furniture, except for the secondhand bed where she was lying with her little son, and an old couch where Gloria slept.

An enormous cockroach crossed the room and hid in the corner. It took her a minute to realize where she was. It had been only a few months since they had moved to this horrendous neighborhood. But at the time, the place had seemed convenient, and it had been all they could find after the tremendous fight with her sister.

"You moved into a lower class district," they told Alexandra at work when she let them know her new address. "You need to get out of there fast."

Alexandra didn't understand what they meant by a lower district. Not until some black kids stole her purse while she was walking down the street, and some others, in the park, attacked her child because he didn't look quite as black as the rest of them, then she knew. It was too dangerous to remain in that area.

She wiped the drops of sweat from her face and looked at the clock: it was 5 a.m. Her little son slept peacefully and so did Gloria. It hadn't been a dream. It was a nightmare come to life, Alexandra thought. If only I hadn't gone to see Jules last night, none of this would be real. But once again a force had compelled her to Jules' door, so she had gone, like the dog goes to his master after being beaten, looking for grace.

Alexandra closed her eyes and felt a chilling tremor remembering the malefic figure of Jules lying lifeless and insipid on the bed the night before. His eyes fixed on the television, inattentive of her presence, then, pushing her and possessing her body violently and releasing her with indifference when he was through.

"What kind of a human being are you?" he had ejected with sinister anger after a half hour of silence. "You look as miserable as if you were going to die standing there in silence. What do you want?"

Alexandra couldn't answer; she had a knot in her throat. Jules was right! She felt like dying of pain because she could not make sense of his cold heart.

"Is sex what you want?" he yelled, rising suddenly and leaning her abruptly against the bed. "Is it?

"I love you," Alexandra had whispered, like a victim in the hands of her oppressor. Then, she screamed, as if her entrails had been cut by a blazing dagger tearing them in million shreds as he possessed her.

"You have to go now." He said, pushing her away and brushing with his hands the wrinkles of the covers that had appeared where he had thrust her. "I am expecting company." He glanced at her with disgust. As he spoke, the bell rang. He combed his hair, straightened his clothing, and rushed to open the door.

"Hi!" Alexandra heard from the bedroom the smiling voice of a woman greeting Jules at the front door.

"Hi!" Jules said fawningly. "I'm ready, let's go."

Seconds later, the front door clicked shut. Jules and the woman were gone leaving her with the full weight of his defilement.

Alexandra stumbled across the room shaking, removed the wet clothes, and went into the cold shower. It had not been a dream. Now she was sure, far from beyond, the ghostly shadow of Nina had come to let her know that she was pregnant.

"It's positive, my dear. You are pregnant." The nurse confirmed Nina's words at the clinic.

Alexandra leaned against the wall not to fall. The circumstances of this pregnancy were the most unfortunate.

"Are you all right?" the nurse asked.
"Yes," she said.

67

The innocent and pure, black eyes of her son were staring at her with sweetness.

"Don't cry, mommy. Don't cry!" Franco pleaded, holding her as his own tears melted with hers, frightened at her despair.

She could not control herself. All she ever wanted when she met Jules was to find the comfort of a true love, yet...,

"Get rid of the baby." Jules had declared with his almost bestial attitude when she went to see him to let him know that she was pregnant. "I don't want it. Do you?"

Perhaps she intuited his reaction, but the lacerating and tearing truth embodied in the sinister, impenetrable, black figure of Jules, when he said that asphyxiated her.

"Sex is for one minute, a child is for a lifetime," she heard him saying remorselessly and brutishly. "Are you ready for that? I am not. You already have Franco."

Alexandra gazed at him with trepidation; it was an absurdity to think that she had been more than once looking at him imploringly, her eyes caressing warmly his cold and imperturbable body. She didn't stay to hear more. She ran away like possessed by a thousand devils feeling a profound revulsion for herself, for having loved him so deeply that she lost all sense of self esteem.

"He is going to let you die alone," Gloria warned her before she decided to go tell him the news.

"Why are you crying, mommy? Tell me!" The despair of her little son's voice shut off her recollection. She held him dearly, still sobbing, and sat him on her lap.

"I'm sad because your daddy doesn't love us."

"I love you, mommy. Don't cry!" Franco said with all the sweetness of his pure and beautiful heart.

"I love you, too, my little darling, more than anybody in this world." She wiped her tears. "Come," she said, "let's go to hear the frogs sing."

They kissed each other, held hands, and walked out into the night.

68

The next few days were for Alexandra like a torture. She had that constant heaviness in her heart; her reason blunted. She needed to talk to someone. The hours were like months, each minute essential.

"If I were you," Alexandra's supervisor said, "I wouldn't hesitate to have an abortion. The man is not worth a peanut!" Alexandra's supervisor had her legs crossed, her right hand on her chin, and she was looking at Alexandra as she talked straight in the eye, with her limpid and sincere blue eyes.

"You are a young and beautiful girl; you don't deserve to tie yourself to someone like that. I am sure that you can find a man that gives you the love and respect that you and your little son need."

Alexandra was sitting in front of her listening carefully. It was good to hear the sound of a friendly voice. Until now, she had been so confused.

Mrs. Rigaud was in charge of the hospital's registration department, and she was the most fair and humanitarian person that Alexandra had ever met. She was around fifty years of age, short, and a little heavy; however, she possessed more energy than a youngster. She loved work, people, and life.

"Go do it tomorrow. I'll give you three days off. If you need more, call and let me know. You need to take care of this as soon as possible."

"Thank you, Mrs. Rigaud," Alexandra said appreciatively.

"It's a hard decision for you, I know," Mrs. Rigaud continued gravely, "but it is the best thing you can do for you and your little son. I would advise my daughter to do the same thing, that man is horrible."

Until she talked to Mrs. Rigaud, she hadn't had any certitude. She had been in a state of constant distress and constant constraint, repelled, at the same time, by the idea of having an abortion, and by the idea of carrying another child of the man who so clearly detested them. There was no way out, Alexandra knew. She wasn't that strong, or at least she didn't feel strong, and the resort was unavoidable. Love, acceptance, want, respect, and concern were some of the fruits of love, not dejection, hate, revulsion, disrespect, and unconcern. Jules felt all these for them.

69

No one was smiling or talking. There was a silence of death in the spacious room. There was fear, coyness, and somber looks that couldn't dissemble the harshness and tension of the oppressive moment. Some teenagers and some adults were all waiting like her before the chamber of death, with a horrible feeling of aloness.

She glanced at the window. Her stomach was constricted and it hurt. It was better not to think. Numb the mind not to feel, to extirpate in that manner the excruciating grief and shame that she felt. Alexandra closed her eyes to escape...

She was with Franco. They had walked down a few blocks hand in hand to the little pond were the frogs sang during the night.

"Shh...! Listen." Alexandra said, stopping a foot away from the little pond. Franco's eyes were shining brightly.

"Look!" He shouted, pointing in the direction of the pond with his little hand.

With her eyes she followed his gesture. Out of nowhere, here and there, as many as twenty frogs came out leaping and gathered rapidly around the pond, singing loudly. The sound was fantastic. This was indeed a magic place. Their magic place, where their imagination could soar as high as the moon shone above their heads.

"They are singing to the moon, 'Shine pretty moon. Shine.'"

"Really?" Franco asked.

"Yes, my little darling, that's the reason they come out--to sing love songs to the moon and to drink water in the pond."

Her lovely child was giving her his undivided attention.

"In the morning when we wake up, they go to sleep."

Franco smiled happily, absolutely fascinated.

Alexandra opened her eyes and looked about again. No one had moved. Everyone in that room seemed to be wrapped in their own lugubrious thoughts. Not even in her wildest dreams had she imagined that one day, she would be in a place like this, as the executioner and as the executed, waiting, still wrestling between right and wrong, shame and pride, survival and extinction, justification and blame. For now there was no reason to evaluate the circumstances anymore. In face of adversity for each person the events and steps to take would be different perhaps in accordance to his or her idea of what is valuable.

"Alexandra Marquez?"

She looked at the nurse with anguish, stood up and followed her.

Two hours later, Alexandra came out of the abortion clinic dragging her body and her soul. The piece of herself she had willfully relinquished had been snatched away.

70

Alexandra couldn't pinpoint exactly when Gloria changed, but her nags became insufferable. She talked to them with haughtiness as if she had reasons to humiliate them.

"Gloria, our living arrangement isn't working anymore. I am moving with Franco to another apartment. I don't like anyone, including you, to mistreat Franco. I have had it with that."

A smirk of anger crossed Gloria's face. "I was going to tell you the same thing. I had already made plans to move. I don't like children, and living alone would be much better for me."

"I'm glad," Alexandra said, tired of explanations.

One week from then, she moved to her new apartment. It was small but it was nice to live by herself with Franco. Peace was all she ever wanted. She had it now, with Franco.

71

Living alone worked marvelously. Her little son attended school while she worked, and on the weekends they went to Metarie, to spend time with Adela and Ronaldo. Mariana didn't live with her brother and sister anymore. Tired of New Orleans, she had gone to San Francisco.

Unlike other Friday evenings, today's trip was special. It was Adela's birthday, and a party had been planned. Franco packed the little present he had wrapped for his aunt, then, they headed to the bus stop. It was a thirty-five minute drive, but riding the bus gave them the opportunity to sightsee in some other parts of the beautiful city of New Orleans. By the time they got to her sister's home, the party was well underway. Some people were swimming, some were eating, and others, were sitting around the pool singing Mexican songs.

It was exciting to listen to Mexican songs again, interpreted by a great voice with the lively sound of guitars. It was so romantic. She wasn't very keen on parties, but this time was different.

"Adela, I was asked to work early in the morning," Alexandra told her sister three hours later. "Is it O.K. if I leave Franco with you and pick him up after work? I don't want to wake him up that early in the morning, nor leave him alone in my house."

"It will be O.K. Don't worry."

"I have an early shift; I will be leaving around 5:00 a.m.

to make it to work on time—I'll pick him up around 4:00 p.m., is that all right?"

"That's fine. Go get some sleep. I have to wait down here until everyone leaves."

Alexandra came towards her sister and hugged her. "Happy birthday!" she said. "Thanks."

179

Adela smiled and went back to the yard where a few people were still dancing. Upstairs, Alexandra knelt down, holding Franco in her arms to say their nightly prayer, then, she put him in bed. She turned the light off and walked towards the window. The night was absolutely marvelous, garnished with a million stars. Down in the yard, the silhouettes still moved to the sound of romantic music.

72

It was still dark when Alexandra left her sister's house. At this hour, the street was solitary. She walked quickly down the street, turning her head to look back from time to time. The bus stop was three blocks away and for some reason she had a feeling of apprehension. This was the first time that she was trying to get from Metarie to New Orleans this early in the morning. I hope the bus comes soon, she thought as she stood at the stop sign. I don't want to be late.

She had an obsession with tardiness. She liked to keep her word, be fair in her dealings, and be a trustworthy and responsible person.

After 20 minutes, there was still not a soul on the street nor a sign of the bus coming. An uneasy feeling started to invade her. Far off, the light of two approaching headlights diminished the darkness. It wasn't the bus; they were car headlights. Nine or ten blocks away from her family's apartments there was a section where the bars remained open all night. Her heart began to pound rapidly. As the car approached, she looked around nervously; there was still no one around.

Where is that bus? Why is it taking so long? She thought. The car continued to approach and her heart pounded harder. The car, as she had feared, stopped in front of her.

"Where are you going, baby? I can give you a ride," said the man in the car with a demanding and almost violent tone.

She glanced at him rapidly, trying to appear calm. The man was in his thirties, wore glasses and he had a vicious look on his face. His hands were moving incessantly on the wheel. She looked up the road. There was still no sign of the bus.

"I told you I can give you a ride. Don't you hear me?" the man screamed.

"Thank you," she answered politely, trying to hide her fear. "I will catch the bus."

The man hit the wheel with his fists, as a perverse grimace distorted his already vicious looks even more.

"If I said I'll give you a ride, it means exactly that! Do you understand?" he said angrily, getting out of the car in one stride, grabbing her, and pushing her inside the car.

Oh no, not this! She thought in anguish as she yelled, taken by surprise.

The man took off at full speed going faster and faster as his free hand fiercely lifted her skirt, touching her and pinching her skin savagely.

"Let me out," she begged as he entered the freeway, trying to release herself from his grasp. "Let me out."

A loud, grotesque laugh came out of his mouth, as his hand like a tendril continued to grasp her flesh, hurting her and filling her with disgust. If she stayed in the car, he was going to kill her, Alexandra knew. She had that cold sweat in her body, that sixth sense of premonition. She needed to escape.

A million thoughts flashed through her mind as the car also sped on the freeway, 70, 75, 80 miles per hour. Her heart was exploding in her chest. She looked around in trepidation. Every minute added a little more to her anxiety. Her son was at her sister's house, unaware of what was happening, waiting for her to pick him up.

By the anger and the ruthless grin the man had on his face, and by the force he had in his hand, it was easy for her to tell she had fallen into the hands of a sadist. She shivered. As long as she stayed in the car, she was his prey. To save herself, she needed to be calm. At no other time, had she experienced such total awareness of her surroundings. Her mind was watchful, alert, focused on each minuscule tension of the man's face, his movements, and the road that was illuminated now by the bright sunlight.

"Let me out, please," she begged again when the man took the bridge that lead to Gretna from New Orleans. Her instinct for survival told her that as long they remained riding on the freeway within town, she still had a chance to be saved. On a desolate country road, where he was probably heading, she wouldn't.

"If you don't let me out of the car, I'll jump." Alexandra said simply.

The man glanced at her momentarily, accelerating more. They were still crossing the bridge and Alexandra had managed, as she said that, to push him away and to open the car door. He was driving so fast that it was hard for her to see the ground clearly. Down below them was the Mississippi river, flowing with magnificence and peace.

"If I jump now," Alexandra thought instantly as she opened the door. "I will get killed. The cars coming behind us will run over me."

The guy pulled her violently towards him as they left the bridge, clamping his hand with even more strength on Alexandra's body. She bit her lips with despair and looked at him out of the corner of her eye in anguish. The guy had a knife hidden in his jacket.

"I need to jump." She thought again, "I can get killed if I do it, but that's the only chance I have to be saved."

Despite these persistent thoughts, she couldn't jump right away. The man was driving in the middle lane, and jumping there would mean an immediate death.

Please, God of mine, Alexandra implored silently, help me to get out of this one! Help me to go back to pick up my son! Just as she thought these words in silence, her assailant jerked the car to the outer lane. "It's now or never," Alexandra said to herself, opening the car door and jumping without further thought into the air.

The impact was so brutal that she rolled down the hill nine or ten times before stopping. The brittle seashells that lay at the sides of the freeway cut into her arms and legs like small blades. For a fraction of a second everything was black; then she stood up, feeling no pain.

"Where am I?" she wondered as she started to climb the hill back to the freeway.

A police officer appeared at the top of the hill and ran towards her. She didn't know where he came from or the reason he was there, but as he ran towards her, he asked, "Did he throw you out of the car? Did he push you?" His face was stricken by a genuine concern.

She stared at him with vague eyes.

"Hurry!" the policeman said, holding her by the arm. "We must not let him get away. We'll chase him! He must not be far!" He helped her inside the police patrol, turned on the siren, and took off at full speed after the assailant's car, that a minute or two ago, with the door still open, had disappeared ahead into the flow of cars.

"No!" Alexandra screamed, terrified. "I don't want to chase him. I am fine. I just want to go back to New Orleans."

The police officer stared at her, astonished, as he continued the chase. "He pushed you. You can press charges. We can apprehend him now."

"He didn't push me." Alexandra said, looking away. "I jumped. I don't want to press any charges, follow him, or apprehend him, I just want to go back to New Orleans."

This time the police officer looked at her suspiciously. Alexandra looked away. He was probably thinking that she was some kind of weirdo, but it didn't matter. The last thing she wanted was publicity, to appear on television, or on the front page of the newspapers. The police would interrogate her and find out that she was an illegal alien, then, they would deport her altogether with her son, her brother and her sister back to Mexico.

"Are you sure that you don't want to press charges?" he insisted, still driving at full speed after the car from which she had jumped.

"I am sure," Alexandra asserted. "Please, let me go."

"I can't let you go like this," said the policeman, irritated. "You are bleeding. The least I can do is to take you to a hospital. If you change your mind, you can still press charges there."

"Thank you. I won't change my mind."

He looked at her with disbelief, then, nodded his head. In his profession he was probably used to meeting all kinds of impertinent oddities. She wasn't one. She just didn't have a legal visa to stay in the country. That was all. Without it, she couldn't complain. Without legal papers, she had to keep a low profile and her mouth shut, taking whatever came in fear of otherwise being discovered and deported.

She had no idea where she was or what hospital he was taking her to. Everything around seemed diffused.

"It's here." The officer said.

He parked the patrol at one side of the emergency door and helped her out of the car. She felt like throwing up.

"Are you all right?" he asked.

"I'm fine." Alexandra replied, controlling her nausea.

The officer walked with her to the front desk.

"This girl jumped out of a car on the freeway," he explained, pointing at her in disbelief. "I brought her to be checked. She doesn't want to press charges. If she changes her mind, take the necessary information. I'll be back later."

Alexandra looked away. She didn't want to meet the officer's eyes. She was scared. The panic she felt to be caught at work, or every time she had gone to look for a job was nothing compared to this.

The officer walked out of the building as a nurse brought her inside the examination room. She felt a sense of relief. What she needed to do now, was say that she was all right so the doctor would let her go back to New Orleans. She still hadn't figured out how she was going to make it. She had no money, she had lost her purse in the car, and she had no idea where she was.

In the examination room, they took some x-rays, gave her some stitches in the wounds she had in her arms and legs and put bandages around them. They worked in silence, staring at her from time to time. When they finished, she resembled a mummy, but she felt no pain except for her hands, which had swollen to almost double their natural size. Her face was untouched. Perhaps instinctively she had covered it when she rolled down. It was hard to figure that out; she didn't remember anything except for the thought that she had to be saved and able to go back to pick up her son.

"Can you lend me twenty-five cents to make a phone call?" she asked the nurse with embarrassment. "I lost my purse in the car, and I have no idea where I am. I am going to call a friend to take me back to New Orleans."

The nurse's thoughts were reflected in her countenance, which indicated that the world out there had turned crazy. For Alexandra, the nurse's reasoning was clear. She must have offered a pathetic and funny view, wearing a ripped and bloody dress, wrapped like a mummy, walking around, affirming that everything was all right and that nothing of major significance had happened. The nurse looked at Alexandra with slight resignation and handed her a quarter.

"Thanks," said Alexandra, diverting her eyes.

She went across the lobby area towards the pay phones, got the receiver, dialed the number, and sent a quick glance toward the front door. Outside, the morning was well advanced by now. She had lost track of the time, but she was at least three hours late for work.

"Hello?"

"Katie?" Alexandra asked. "I am sorry to bother you, I was in an accident this morning. I am in a hospital somewhere across the bridge in Gretna. I was wondering if you could come to pick me up. I... I have no idea of how to get back to New Orleans. I lost my purse." Her voice was fast and nervous even though she had tried hard to sound natural.

Alexandra heard a silence at the other end of the line and then the disconcerted voice of her friend. "What hospital? What's the name of this hospital?"

"I don't know. Let me ask," she answered. "Just a moment."

Alexandra met Katie at Touro Infirmary. Katie worked part time in the evenings and attended Louisiana State University in the mornings. Switching working hours is how they had met. Katie was a black girl of about twenty-two years of age.

"Excuse me, can you tell me the name of this hospital?" Alexandra asked. The woman passerby stopped for a brief second and gave her the name of the hospital.

"I am in the Jo Ellen Hospital," Alexandra told her friend.

"O.K. I know where it is. I'll be there in twenty minutes."
"Thanks. I'll be waiting for you at the front door."
"O.K."

Alexandra hung up the phone, twice as nervous. She knew that Katie hadn't believed her story. Her accident was too unlikely. She lived in New Orleans; if she had an accident on her way to work, what in the world was she doing in a hospital in another city?

After a few minutes, Katie pulled up in front of the hospital door.

"Hi!" Alexandra greeted her friend happily as she opened the car door and jumped in.

Katie's eyes widened as her mouth dropped open in surprise.

"What happened to you?" Katie asked, pulling away.

"Don't ask," Alexandra said, embarrassed.

"Well?"

"If I tell you, you won't believe it. I don't believe it, either."

Katie's eyebrows lifted.

"A guy abducted me this morning, but before he could do anything to me, I jumped out of his car on the freeway."

Katie looked her in the eye incredulously.

"I can't go to work with all these bandages." Alexandra continued.

"Of course you can't." Katie interrupted, appalled at what she had heard.

"Could you please let them know, when you go there, that I had an accident and that is the reason I didn't show up to work?"

"I will tell them, don't worry."

"Please, don't tell them what really happened. It's so embarrassing. I don't want anyone to know."

"Girl, you did nothing. What are you concerned about?"

"Nothing. I just don't want them to know." She remained silent for a few seconds, then, she added, "I need to go to my sister's house. She lives in Metarie; my son is there," she explained.

"Tell me which way to go."

Alexandra gave her directions, and the rest of the trip was done in silence. Katie's silence indicated that she wanted more explanations, but Alexandra couldn't tell her any more. Everything she wanted to disclose of the matter had been disclosed, even if it didn't make that much sense.

"It's here!" she exclaimed enthusiastically when they got in front of her sister's apartment complex. "Here, by the side of the street. Thanks, I appreciate your kindness."

"You are welcome," her friend answered politely. "I hope you feel better."

"I'm fine, don't worry." She hugged Katie and jumped out of the car with great relief. Just a few hours ago she couldn't tell for sure if she was going to make it back.

"What happened?" her sister and son screamed, terrified, as if they had seen an apparition the moment they opened the door.

"It's nothing. I'm fine," Alexandra said, sitting down with dismay. "Don't worry."

"What do you mean don't worry. You have all these bandages. What happened?" Adela asked.

Alexandra laughed nervously, telling in a few words what she had been through.

"I can't believe it, Alexandra. It's a miracle that you are alive and all right." Adela said.

"God helped me to save myself, that's all. I'm fine, a little sore, but I'll be fine."

"Are you sure, mommy?" Franco asked, holding her with his ever touching concern and sensitivity.

"Yes, my little sweetheart, mommy is fine. Let's not talk about it anymore." She kissed her little boy several times, then she added, "We'll stay here for the day, but tomorrow morning we'll go back to New Orleans."

Her sister Adela watched in silence. "I am not working now. I'll go back with you," she said.

"I was so afraid when I saw the police officer." Alexandra said. "I thought that I was going to be on the news if I pressed charges, and that all of us would be deported."

"I know," her sister said quietly.

"I am going to bed," Alexandra said.

"I am going to the store to get some groceries. I'm taking Franco with me. We'll be back."

"O.K." Alexandra said, yawning. All of a sudden the only thing she wanted was to sleep and rest, and forget the stiffness and soreness of her muscles.

"Mrs. Rigaud? This is Alexandra. I am not going to be able to go to work for a few days; I had an accident and I am a little sore. I'm sorry."

"Don't worry dear, I understand. Katie told us how badly you were hurt. I am going to give you two weeks sick leave, so you can take care of yourself. Will that be enough?"

"Mrs. Rigaud, it will be more than enough. Thank you very much."

"You're welcome. Your health comes first. Call me if you need more time."

"I will, Mrs. Rigaud. Thank you again. Bye."

"Bye, dear."

Alexandra hung up with relief. At least, that had been taken care of. She was concerned about her job, but for the moment, in the condition she was in, she couldn't go to work. The immense black bruise on her buttocks didn't let her sit down or even lay down on her back. It hurt terribly, along with the deep uncertainty and uneasiness that had fallen over her about any further consequences that the event could bring her. The maniac had her purse in the car, thus he knew her name and where she worked by the work badge that she always carried. Would he be looking for her, right at that moment, to finish what he had started? She couldn't disregard that possibility, and the thought bothered her tremendously. There was, however, one positive thing: the maniac didn't know her home address--at least, not her real address. At work, except for her name and social security number, all the information she had given was false. Without having a legal status in the country, it was wise to take precautions to protect her whereabouts. Thereby, no conclusive clues existed to track her down in case someone became suspicious of her illegal status.

The shrill ring of the phone distracted her thoughts and startled Franco, who was watching television in the living room.

"Hello?"

"Hello, beautiful!" an unmistakable voice greeted her at the other end of the line. "How is it going?"

"Hi Warren, how are you doing?" She couldn't contain her joy and surprise.

"I asked first." The masculine voice was emotional.

"We... are fine," Alexandra lied.

"Really? You don't sound so convincing," Warren said. "You can always come back to Utah if you are not doing well down there, you know that," he invited.

"Yes, I know. Thank you," she acknowledged nervously.

"In fact, why don't you?" he said. "Alysjo and I have been talking about it. We miss you, and the kids miss you, too. You guys will meet my little one--the one that we were expecting when you left over a year ago."

"Yes, I remember. How is he?"

"He is adorable."

"I imagine so. Well, I am glad."

"You haven't answered me. Are you coming back?"

"Warren, it wouldn't be right. It would be too much imposition for you and Alysjo to have us there again. My sister Adela is with me now."

"Alexandra, if you want to come back, my house is always open for you and your family. It will be all right with Alysjo. Just let me know if you decide."

"I'll think about it."

"You are too far away. Come back... here I can take care of you all."

It was as if he had sensed that they were in danger and had called to offer them the alternative they needed. Right now, she wasn't well. Even when she appeared calm in front of Adela and her little son, it was an act. Her sole purpose was not to put any strain on them, but out of their sight she was in great distress. She feared constantly that at any moment she could meet the maniac on the street to take her with him again.

"Tell me that you are coming back," Warren insisted. "You'll get a job up here. This is a safe place, safer than New Orleans."

"All right," she assented. "We'll go back."

She heard his pleasant laugh. "Good, good. That sounds much better. Your little fellow will be happier here."

"Are you sure it'll be okay with Alysjo? I don't want to go back there to cause trouble."

"She is right here, at my side. You can ask her yourself."

Suddenly she heard Alysjo.

"Alexandra, it will be fine." Alysjo said. "That's why we called you. We were thinking about you, and we felt that you would be better off out here."

"Thank you, Alysjo. I have caused you so much trouble. I really appreciate your kindness."

"Here is Warren," she said.

"See? I told you. It will be fine, beautiful."

"If you say so."

"When you get here, just call. We'll come to pick you up at the sound of your voice."

"We'll let you know. It'll take us one or two weeks to get ready."

"O.K. We'll be looking forward to seeing you soon. Bye now."

"Bye. Thank you."

Without thinking she had accepted, motivated perhaps by the thought of the maniac who was roaming loose somewhere, and also by the desire she had to mitigate all the bad memories that New Orleans brought her. She went up to her son and hugged him.

"We are going back," she told him when he was in her arms.

"Where, mommy?" He asked, surprised.

"To Utah, my sweetie. Warren called. He wants us to go back. I wasn't going to accept, but after what happened to me, I think it is better to go back there. I don't feel safe here anymore."

"It's understandable. I wouldn't feel save either." Adela replied from the kitchen. "Did you hear Franco? We are going to Utah."

"When are we leaving, mom?"

"Next week."

"I like Utah, mom. I will be able to play with my friends again."

"Yes, you will. The schools are nicer there. Do you remember your teacher, how nice she was, and how much she loved you?"

"Yeah."

73

With a trembling hand, Alexandra dialed Jules number. She didn't really know why she was doing it; perhaps to see him one more time. She was leaving New Orleans and this time she knew it was for good.

"Hello?" she heard Jules say.

"Jules? This is Alexandra. I am sorry to bother you at this time of the night, but we are leaving New Orleans tonight, and I wanted to ask you if you could give us a ride to the bus station."

There was silence.

"Are you there? Jules?"

"What time?" He finally asked.

"In about an hour," she said. "The bus leaves at midnight."

"Where are you going?"

"To Utah."

Silence followed.

I'll be there," He said without further comment and hung up.

Alexandra stared at the receiver for a few seconds in silence. He hadn't been surprised by her call, or if he had, she couldn't tell. She shook her head, hung up, and stood up. She did not want to remember.

Adela and Franco were out in the yard counting the stars and listening to melodies being sung by the neighborhood crickets. Like two bright stars, Franco's eyes were always opened in wonder and amazement, alert to his surroundings. He was certainly going to miss the lizards, the snails, the frogs, the buzzing beetles, the short expeditions they took in search of four leaf clovers, and his toys that they had given away in order to travel with less difficulty.

"What did Jules say?" Adela asked. "Is he going to take us to the bus station or did he refuse? That guy is absolutely hateful!"

"He'll be here," Alexandra said. "I hope."

They put the luggage at the top of the stairs, and sat on the floor to wait for Jules. At 11:30 p.m., he came. He grabbed their luggage in silence and put it inside the trunk of his new Cadillac. When he finished, he turned to them.

"Shall we?"

They assented and got into the car.

In the car Alexandra couldn't help but gaze at his profile. It was like an impassible mask, with no other expression but the indestructible barrier he always put between them. But the memories were still there, afflicting her soul with heaviness and grief. Since she had known him, he had destroyed, one by one, all of her dreams.

When they got to the station, it was close to midnight, but despite the late hour, the bus station was swarming with people. Alexandra gazed around nervously. The roar of the nearby engines was a clear indication that in just a few more minutes all would be behind. Jules at a short distance like the bronze statue she had always seen, insensitive waiting for their departure.

The passengers had formed a line to board the bus, and some were pushing their way in. She turned her head to look at him. One last look and that was all--not even one word of goodbye.

The bus smelled like sweat and dirt. It was packed, but right now it didn't matter. She sat and held her son tightly, trying to calm the pounding of her heart. She needed to survive. Utah or any other place at this point wouldn't make any difference. She put on her sweater, shivering. A minute later, the bus dashed into the night. She didn't know why, but inside herself something was being crushed again with a pain similar to a million tiny thorns sticking all at once into her body, her brain, and her soul. Like a vague shadow, the city of New Orleans was disappearing behind.

Outside in the dark sky the moon shone plain like a giant lantern. She needed to forget. Time and distance were the best medicine, along with the challenge of a new beginning.

IN UTAH

From almost 100 degrees in New Orleans, the temperature went down to 24 degrees in Utah, and it was snowing. Alexandra took off her sweater and gave it to Franco. She left Franco with her sister by the door of the bus station, where it was dry, and went to the nearest paid phone to call Warren.

The bus station, at this hour of the night, was closed. Everything was pitch black except for the fresh resplendent snow covering the ground.

"Hello?"

"Warren, we are here, at the bus station. Can you come to pick us up?"

"It will take me fifteen to twenty minutes," said Warren yawning.

"I am sorry to wake you up."

"No problem. I'll be there."

"Thanks." She hung up. The wind was blowing madly and it was freezing.

"What a change!" Adela said, shivering. "Who would have guessed? Snow on the last day of May? It's incredible."

"Yeah, but everything is possible with the weather in Utah." Alexandra said as she sat on the floor near Franco and covered him with her arms, attempting to warm him a little.

"Did you get hold of Warren?"

"Yeah, he'll be here in a few minutes."

"He is nice to have asked us to come."

"Yeah." Alexandra acknowledged. "But we can't stay in his house for long. We need to find a way to move out of there as soon as possible. He is married, and we are coming here to interfere in his life again."

"I agree with you; we have to move as soon as possible."

Alexandra made no more comments. The three days they had spent riding the bus had been exhausting. The only thing she wanted to do was to get to the nearest bed, put Franco to bed, and sleep.

The roar of Warren's truck cut into her wandering thoughts and tracked the untouched snow over the ground.

"Hi there," said Warren, jumping out of the truck and picking up their luggage. "Hurry! Get in. You guys are freezing; what happened to your coats?"

"It was 99 degrees in New Orleans. We didn't know you still had snow out here. We don't have any," Adela explained.

"You must be freezing. You'll get warm now. I have a good heater in this truck."

He pulled out of the bus station carefully. The road was very slick. "You'll be surprised to know who is here," he said.

"Who?" Alexandra and Adela asked.

"Your sister Mariana and her son," he explained. "They got here a week ago," he continued. "She said she called the hospital where you worked in New Orleans, and they told her you quit because you were moving out here."

Alexandra and Adela gazed at each other mortified. He had offered his home to them, but not to the whole family.

"Warren, I am sorry, we didn't know she was here." Alexandra said, shocked. "If we would had known she was here, we wouldn't have come. Not at this time, at least. I think it is a little bit too much for you and Alysjo to have us all here depending on you at the same time."

"Alexandra," Warren said, looking at her with reproach, "you and your family will always be welcome in my house. You know I would do anything for you."

Alexandra and Adela looked at each other in embarrassment.

"Thanks," Alexandra said, not knowing what else to say.

75

They saw Alysjo in the morning; her resentment was plain. All of a sudden her husband had taken away her privacy by asking five strangers to invade her house, and that was hard to understand. Alexandra didn't blame her; Warren would be supporting them all, and perhaps, deep inside, Alysjo understood her husband's real motives for having them there. That's why she had avoided Warren since the moment they arrived. For three weeks it had been like hide and seek. She leaving the room when he came in, or engaging with someone else in conversation whenever he was present. However, she hadn't been able to avoid the blaze in Warren's eyes that was directed at her, making her nervous.

"Alexandra," Alysjo called from upstairs that evening. "Daniel is here to see you."

"I'm coming," she answered.

Daniel Cartwright and Warren were friends; he had come to visit a couple of times and had stayed for dinner.

"Hi," Alexandra said, coming upstairs, surprised.

"Hello," Daniel greeted her, smiling. "I wanted to invite you to go to the canyon to see my horses. Would you like to come?"

Alexandra glanced at her sisters and Alysjo nervously.

"Go," Alysjo encouraged her. "Daniel is very impressed with you. The horses are only fifteen minutes away from here. It's a nice ride. We won't be having dinner for another hour."

Alexandra looked at Alysjo, then at Daniel. Daniel was strong and genteel. He appeared to be seven feet tall. His hair was red, muscular and quite handsome. His eyes were tremendously green. At this moment he was looking at her with an open, frank, and appealing smile.

She hesitated for a minute and then she smiled, "All right," Alexandra said. "I'll be back."

76

It was dark when they came back. The ride took longer than they had expected and everybody in the house had finished dinner. Franco and Sean were playing dominos with Warren's kids, her sisters were downstairs, and Warren and Alysjo were watching the news.

"Hi," she said shyly, coming in with Daniel.

"Hi, buddy," Daniel said stepping in and patting Warren's shoulder.

"Hi," Warren answered a little uptight. "Where did you go? we waited for you for half hour before we had dinner."

"I am sorry," Daniel apologized. "I took Alexandra to ride one of my horses, and then we decided to get something to eat. You don't mind, do you?"

Warren's face was a little crossed. "Of course I don't."

"I like Alexandra you know." Daniel stated with appalling simplicity.

A grimace crossed Warren's face. "I know."

"Well," Alexandra said nervously, "thanks for the invitation and the hamburger Daniel. Goodnight."

"Good night." Daniel said, kissing her hand.

Alexandra went across the room followed by the attentive look of Alysjo, who hadn't said a word.

"Good night," she said, then, ran downstairs.

"Alexandra!"

Alexandra turned and looked at Warren, surprised. He had caught up with her at the bottom of the stairs.

"Yes?"

"What did he tell you?" Warren's voice was filled with anxiety.

"Who?"

"Daniel--where did he take you?"

201

She blushed. "He said he likes me, and that he wants to marry me."

"I know that. He told that to Alysjo the other day, but what did you say to him? Are you going to marry him?"

She breathed deeply. "I don't know--he is nice, but I don't know."

"Tell me that you won't accept. Tell me that you won't marry him," he said, grasping her by the arms, his voice sounding hoarse and doleful. "Tell me that you won't go out with him anymore. Tell me!"

"Warren... I--" she whispered, confused, looking down.

"Tell me!" he demanded, staring at her anxiously.

"Warren, Alysjo is upstairs."

"Tell me!" His skin was red and his voice was shaking in jealousy and desperation.

"Warren, are you down there?" Alysjo called at the top of the stairs. She was pregnant again, and her house was even messier than the first time Alexandra had lived with them.

The masculine eyes were imploring.

"I won't... I won't accept," she said nervously.

Warren released her. His face had a grin of relief and his eyes showed the love he felt for her.

"Goodnight," he said, going upstairs.

Alexandra sighed. "We need to get out of here as soon as possible," she said to herself.

77

"Alexandra, Daniel is here to see you," Alysjo screamed from the top of the stairs the following day.

Alexandra got a knot in her chest, but she went upstairs running. Warren had come home early that evening, motivated perhaps because of Daniel. She passed by Warren, who stood in silence near the kitchen, and went towards Daniel.

"Hi," Daniel said smiling, holding her hand as he came halfway to meet her. "I am going to borrow this nice lady for a few minutes and then I'll bring her back," he said loudly.

Warren didn't answer.

"I'll be back in a couple of hours," Alexandra said to Franco and her sisters.

Daniel, holding her by the hand, took her outside.

"Where would you like to go?" he asked.

"Wherever you want."

"Let's get some hamburgers, then, let's go to my apartment. I'll show you where I live. Is that all right?"

"Yes."

Daniel drove for twenty minutes, stopped on the way at a Mc Donald's then, drove to his apartment. He helped her out of the truck, pulled the keys out of his pocket, opened the door and moved one step back to let her in.

"Wow!" Alexandra exclaimed. "This is so pretty!"

"Thanks." Daniel said without any vanity.

She walked through out the apartment, admiring the rustic but exquisite decoration.

"Well," Daniel began, holding her hand, "did you think about what I asked you last night?" He sat on the carpet and pulled her towards him.

"I did." Alexandra answered, sitting by him.

"And?"

"And I can't accept."

"Why not?" Daniel asked.

"I just I barely know you Daniel. I couldn't marry you without love."

Daniel remained quiet for a couple of seconds.

"It's Warren, isn't it?" His voice sounded upset.

She said nothing.

"He is in love with you too, isn't he?" Daniel pursued. "I noticed it the day I met you. It's so obvious he can't hide it! He is so in love, that he is losing it."

Alexandra raised her eyes and looked at Daniel, not knowing exactly what he meant, and blushed.

"He had the nerve to come to my house this morning to ask me if I kissed you last night and to stop seeing you. Can you believe that?" Daniel said angrily.

"I am sorry, Daniel. I didn't know he came here."

"I told him to mind his own damn business and I sent him to hell." Daniel said. "We were close to a fist fight. We didn't, because until now, we have been good friends. Otherwise..." He closed his fists with fury.

"Daniel," Alexandra stammered, feeling very uncomfortable. "I don't want to bring you any complications. I am living at Warren's house. I think it's better if you take me back. I know your address and phone number; when I move to my own apartment, I will give you a call."

"Whatever you wish," Daniel said, still upset as he drank his soda. "Let's finish our hamburgers first. But remember," he pointed at her with his index finger, "I will be waiting for your call. I like you and your son a lot, and I want to marry you." He paused. "I am not playing any games with you. If you agree to marry me, we can go back to Wyoming at the end of the year. You'll like it up there. I have more horses than the ones you saw here, some acres of land...and a beautiful house that I am sure you and your little son would enjoy."

"Thanks, Daniel. I'll think about it," she said, "now, take me home."

His offer was tempting. It would mean the immediate solution to all her problems, but as she told him, she could never marry anybody without love. Also, she had promised Warren that she wouldn't.

78

Finally they got a job. Ten days later, they were ready to move out from Warren's house. While they were having breakfast Alexandra hit them with the news.

"We are moving today. We are very grateful for the trouble of having us here again for so long. Without you, we couldn't have made it."

Alysjo breathed a sigh of relief. "Where are you moving?"

"We are moving to Provo," Mariana answered her without looking at Warren. "It is about time."

"Yes, it is." Adela added. "Thank you very much for having us in your home for so long Alysjo, and excuse us for disrupting your privacy."

"Yes, it's true, thank you. You have been so patient and kind," Alexandra echoed.

"We like it here! Do we have to move again?" Sean and Franco added, disappointed.

"Yes, we are moving, but not very far away from here, so it won't be difficult to come to visit sometimes," Alexandra explained to the kids, who still seemed displeased.

"Have you packed everything?" Alysjo asked. "If you have, I can take you there right away." The tone of her voice was urgent. She couldn't hide her desire to have them out at once before something could happen that would make them change their minds.

"I'll take them," Warren said, who until now had remained silent. "After I help them move, I am going to go to work and won't be back until four thirty."

"Warren, I want to help them move. I want to see their apartment," Alysjo insisted.

"Alys, I'm going to go straight to work after that, and I can't bring you back. I'll show you where they moved some other time." Saying that, he stood up abruptly and turned to Mariana. "Shall we get your things?"

79

Their apartment was nicely carpeted and fully furnished. It had two bedrooms, and for the price, it was an excellent deal. Warren deposited the last piece of luggage on the floor.

"Well girls, here you are--all set."

"Yes, here we are. We owe it all to you, Warren. Thank you!" Mariana exclaimed.

Alexandra was standing in the kitchen in silence. She had been avoiding Warren since the last time he had addressed her in his house when she went out with Daniel.

"Don't leave yet," Sean and Franco begged climbing on his lap and shoulders. "Play with us."

"Some other time, little fellows." He laughed and lifted them by one leg into the air. "I have to go to work now, but I'll come back again soon." He left Sean and Franco wrestling on the sofa, and walked towards Alexandra with that tenderness in his eyes that said all of what his words couldn't.

"Call me if you need anything. I will always be there for you. Don't forget that."

"I know, Warren, thank you," she said, avoiding his eyes.

"I'll be going now." He moved towards the door. "Bye, you guys!" he called in a loud voice. "Good luck!"

"Bye!" Franco, Sean, Mariana, and Adela answered.

80

One week later Alexandra was washing dishes when Warren came. She was alone in the apartment. Her sisters had gone to work, and Franco and Sean were at school.

"Hi there," he greeted, smiling. "How is life treating you?" He was affable and attentive, as if nothing were more important for him than to hear her answer at that moment.

"Fine," she answered nervously, letting him in.

"Where is everyone?" he asked, walking around the room.

"Gone," she answered, raising her shoulders, "to school, to work."

"My men are waiting for me outside," he explained, pacing from one side to another as if all of a sudden he had become tense. "I better be going...I came to check if..." he stared in her eyes. "If...everything was O.K."

"Everything is fine, thank you."

Then without saying more, nervously he rushed out of the apartment as though he had remembered something urgent, but he was still turning his head to stare at her as he walked away.

Like the first time she lived in Utah, Warren came to visit everyday. He made his stops a routine, twice a day: on his way to work in the morning, and on his way back from work in the evening. There was no way to control his visits. Whenever he came he sat in the living room, played with the kids for a while, or wrestled with them on the carpet, always laughing with that authentic, happy, absolutely appealing laugh of his.

"Hey, beautiful!" he always said to Alexandra. "How do you keep this place so attractive? It is so pleasant to come here."

As a rule his co-workers waited outside, but occasionally, he came in with one or two of them. They were strong, huge, blond, and bearded mountain-like men, just like Warren. They stared at her silently sometimes with undisguised lust. Men for some reason felt attracted to her and their presence made her uneasy.

"I'll be back later." Warren said as he opened the door and stepped out followed by the men.

She assented closing the door.

81

Living in Utah was placid. There were not many complications. It was a safe place to live, and Sean and Franco had a lot of friends. She opened the window and gazed at the mountains that surrounded the valley offering such a splendid view. They have been in that apartment for seven months and the mountains always seemed to be dyed with pink when the sun sank behind the lake every evening. Warren hadn't come for a few weeks. That's why, when the bell rang that evening, the last thing she expected was to see him. He looked disastrous. The white shirt he was wearing was unbuttoned, he hadn't shaved, seemed tired, and his black hair fell shaggily over his forehead.

"Hi," he said. "May I come in?"

She opened the door widely. "Are you all right?"

Warren didn't answer. He stepped in and sat in silence on the couch, and for a moment hid his face with his hands. Alexandra knew exactly what his silence meant. The man loved her completely. His eyes had told her so many times. She bit her lips nervously.

"It is beyond me!" he declared suddenly as he stood up and in two strides he reached for her. "I love you!" he said fervently, taking her in his arms. "I need you."

There was no chance to escape from his embrace. Before she knew it, he carried her in his arms into the living room, and sat on the couch with her on his lap.

"I don't have any doubt about this, Alexandra, you hear me? I love you." His eyes were clear, limpid, and secure.

"Warren, I love you, too, but--"

He held her close and kissed her with all the love and passion that he felt for her. His face was tinted with blush, and his pupils were wide, sparkling with glittering light.

"I am going to divorce Alysjo. I can't go on being married to her loving you like this."

"Warren," Alexandra began, "I love you too, but I don't want to be the apple of discord between Alysjo and you. I don't want to be the woman in your life who comes and destroys in one minute what took you years to build: your house, your marriage, and your kids."

"I'll take care of them," he said, "but I want you and need to be with you."

"I would like to be with you too, Warren," she said, frightened, "but I couldn't be happy knowing that you gave up everything that you love and stand for because of me."

"I can handle it," he said firmly. "I am going to tell her. I have decided."

"No! We can't do this to her; she is having your baby, and I can't do this to you either. Not after you have helped me. I cannot return your favor by destroying you like this."

"Alexandra, I have thought it over, and over. Leave it up to me." He smiled with tenderness, touched by her fired concern. "Everything will be all right."

"Warren it won't be all right. They will excommunicate you from the church," she protested.

"I can take it," he said, amazingly serene. "It has been hell like this." He brought her closer to him, caressing her hair, her back, kissing her in silence.

"Please go...don't tempt me; go now before I build my happiness destroying yours." Alexandra was truly frightened. It could have been so easy to shut off the scruples of her mind, and lay with him in ecstasy, in his loving arms that had been there for her at all times. She would have liked to marry him, but not like this—hurting him, the kids, and Alysjo.

He had a look of worry, but he smiled.

"All right," he said, standing up. "I'll go, for now."

82

The next morning the bangs at the door startled her.

"I'm coming, I'm coming!" Alexandra screamed putting a dress on and rushing to the door.

She opened the door and Warren's wife stepped in, crying. Her eyes were swollen and she looked devastated.

"I can't believe that you have done this to me, crawling all over my husband and throwing yourself upon his arms behind my back!" She wiped her nose. "I opened the doors of my house to you and to your family. I helped you! I trusted you, and you pay me back like this: going after my husband and trying to take him away from me." She was crying inconsolably. "How could you do that? Aren't you embarrassed trying to deprive some innocent kids from their dad?"

Alexandra grew pale. "Wait a minute! You have it all wrong, Alysjo," Alexandra said, upset. "I am not after your husband. If I wanted to take your husband away from you, I would have done it a long time ago, but I am not that kind of a person." She paused and breathed deeply meeting Alysjo's eyes. "Your husband loved me since he was on his mission. It didn't start when I was in your house. You are his wife, and I respect that. I have no intentions of taking your husband away from you and destroying your family. I told him that."

"His workers told me that he comes to your house everyday and stays with you for hours at a time."

"Alysjo, I can't help that. If your husband comes to knock at my door, I am going to open it for him."

"How can you do this behind my back? How dare you?"

"Alysjo," Alexandra said, making monumental efforts to remain calm, "I have nothing else to discuss with you. If you have anything else to discuss, go and discuss it with your husband." she paused. "If I were you, I would go back to my home, trust my husband, and forget about this. I am not going to hurt you. I am not going to take your husband away from you. I wouldn't do this to you, to him, or to your kids. I told Warren that, and now I am telling you. I love him too much to take away from him all that was important to him before I came."

Alysjo, who hadn't moved from the spot she took when she came in, remained silent for a few minutes, looking at Alexandra with a distrustful, unconvinced face. She was the portrait of pain. Pale and disheveled as she was, Alysjo depicted a woman who depended totally and entirely upon another human being for subsistence, namely, her husband. Staring at her was for Alexandra like a moment of revelation. Despite the difficult nature of single motherhood and its inherent perils, she had one advantage; she was independent and free. Her security did not depend upon anybody else's effort, but upon her own.

"Warren said--" Alysjo began.

"Your concerns are unfounded," Alexandra cut in. "Nothing has happened between your husband and I. Nothing will. If I were you, I would go back to my husband and love him, love him like he deserves to be loved. You have a very nice and loving husband. I have decided to move to Salt Lake City, and with that, I'll be out of the way. I don't think that your husband will be able to drive everyday to Salt Lake to see me."

When Alysjo left, Alexandra breathed with relief. The encounter had given her a headache. She didn't know what really had happened to precipitate Alysjo's reaction, but it wasn't hard to figure out that Warren had told her about them. "It is too late for us, Warren," she whispered to herself, recalling Warren's loving eyes and Alysjo's anguish. Moving to Salt Lake would make Warren come back to reason. She hated the idea of harming others to be happy. It was over. She couldn't accept him in her life no matter how lonely she felt, or how much she loved him.

83

"Alysjo says you are moving to Salt Lake City." Warren was in front of her in disbelief. There was pain in every feature of his face.

Why was he torturing her? Alexandra thought, didn't he know that even though she also loved him, she was bound by her principles to deny herself of his presence and his love?

"Yes, we are." Alexandra said, in low voice, looking away. Having him in front of her was like being at a dead end with no way out. It would have been so easy to fall right there in his arms.

"Alexandra, I don't want you to move," he said in distress.

She stared at him quickly. He appeared utmost attractive even in this moment of disillusionment. "Please go," she pleaded. "Go back to your wife."

"I'll stay with Alysjo if you want. I won't come to bother you anymore, but don't leave, don't move to Salt Lake. You'll get lost up there. It's a big city."

She gazed at him, wounded and blushing to the end of her ears. If she stayed, they would fall into each other's arms. "Warren, I am moving, and when I do, you will forget about me, you'll see." She looked at him firmly. "You'd better be going now, or the men waiting for you out there, will tell Alysjo that you came here again this evening, and you will have more trouble at home than what you already have."

He stared at her, refusing to believe what he was hearing. His eyes were warm, dilated. "Is this what you want?"

"Yes," she answered seriously. "This is what I want. You are married. Your place is with your wife and with your kids, not with me."

Warren opened his mouth as if he was to say something, but he didn't. He grabbed her arms forcefully and looked into her eyes in silence for a few seconds, then released her. He turned on his heel slowly, and Alexandra heard his measured steps fading away.

She lingered at the window and wearily glanced at the horizon. It was too tiring to move again, but moving, had become a familiar and endless routine in her life.

Warren was now getting inside his truck.

"Goodbye, loving friend." She whispered.

She stayed immobile by the window. Her eyes were now lost into the infinite. Until now she had lived a nomadic life, in her circumstance, without having a real identity and a real establishment that was all she could do. Since she came to the United States, survival had been her basic need, and that's all she had been doing.

"Tomorrow. Maybe all my dreams will come true tomorrow," she whispered imploring in her heart for miracles.

She stepped out the apartment door. Her son was playing with some kids outside, chasing bubbles, and with her hands she tried to touch them. They twinkled like a rainbow of lights in the twilight. For a moment, inside each of those colorful bubbles, she could clearly see herself dancing together with her son to the tune of glorious sounds, free from pain and fulfilling all of her dreams. She shook her head. The bubbles had evaporated, dissolved by the wind.

SEBASTIAN

"Alexandra, you never go out anywhere. Come on, get yourself together, and go with me to the party. I have no one else to go with, and I want to go!" Mariana was insistent.

"O.K., O.K. I'll go with you, but only this time." Alexandra said. "You know how much I hate going to parties, and how much I hate leaving Franco alone when I don't have to go to work."

"I know, but one time won't hurt you. Adela will take care of Franco and Sean, and going to a party will be good for you. Who knows? You might enjoy yourself tonight."

Only five days had passed since they moved from Provo to Salt Lake City, and the party that night had been perhaps the call of fate.

He came from across the dancing room as soon as he caught sight of them and introduced himself, secure and charming. In that instant, when he said, "Hi, I'm Sebastian," Alexandra looked at him benumbed by the firm, well-built flesh of his body, his metallic hazel eyes, his thick beard, and black hair. Nothing is unpleasant about him, she thought. The man had a confident manner and such extravagant and exaggerated movements when he talked that she laughed for the first time unrestrained.

For Alexandra it was like love at first sight. She wanted to find love and to be loved. Forget all about past sorrows.

"Are you married?" Sebastian asked, taking her as they danced outside where the clear rays of moonlight bathed the valley and the mountain slopes.

"I am divorced," Alexandra lied, looking away as she bit her lips.

She knew that if she confessed she was a single mother it would give him a bad impression. Marriage, it had been her experience, provided women with an air of seriousness, protection, and prestige. To say that she had never been married was to be looked on by all, as a low life and a loose soul. No matter which way she looked at it, social status, recognition, and respect, in an almost global patriarchal world, were given by men.

"How can I be so lucky as to meet you?" They were still dancing, and he looked at her warmly, squeezing her hand.

"How can I?" she smiled playfully, not knowing what he was up to.

"Can I see you again tomorrow?"

He had made such a good impression on her that Alexandra wouldn't mind seeing him again, and again. "Yes," she agreed.

"Good," he said, smiling.

He walked to the nearby water fountain and drank with delight. His white shirt was damp with sweat outlining his virile chest.

"You made a conquest!" Mariana teased her when they left the party.

"Please, don't start. It's nothing."

"I think it is something. The guy looked quite interested in you. Did you give him your address?"

"Yes, I did."

"He's not bad, not bad at all."

"See what you've caused?"

"It was about time. You are a hermit."

They didn't talk more, but the cards had been set. That was the beginning of her romance with Sebastian.

A week later, she got a job at a hospital sterilizing surgical instruments, and also started dating Sebastian.

Working in the hospital was nice, but she continued to fill out more applications with the idea of getting a better job. She had set the goal in her mind to work for Enterprises 2000. The benefits were numerous and the pay higher than most companies in Salt Lake. Luckily, three months after she filed her application, Enterprises 2000 called her for an interview, and she was hired.

Despite the success of her endeavor, she wasn't happy. Working without papers in Utah often subjected her to insults and put-downs that she had to take without being able to protest. It wasn't the most comfortable situation to be in, but this was part of the gamble she had taken coming to another country without legal papers--she was a worker without rights. She had to take what came, in order to subsist. However, she didn't remember hearing those put downs on the East Coast. People there were too busy and too much involved in their own groups to notice someone else. "Live and let live" seemed to be their rule, and even though it sounded cold and harsh, it was a better option.

"A great man is never disturbed by a little man," her father always said trying to implant in their minds the wisdom of Socrates. However, every time she heard the prosaic remarks--it was very hard for her to remain impassive.

"No, not a foreigner!" she often heard at work when she answered the phone to customers, "I did not call to hear a damn foreigner! Why don't you go back to your country? Give me someone who speaks English."

Ignorance is certainly darkness, she thought. Regardless, their inordinate frequency of comments like these, she could never get accustomed to them. There was no way that she could embrace the idea that someone could claim superiority and at the same time be unable to care about, and have respect for other individuals.

85

"I don't anticipate marriage," Sebastian told her the day they met, and also five months later, when he took her to meet his children. "But we can have a good and comfortable relationship." It was three in the afternoon and he was driving as he talked.

Sebastian had four children--three teenage boys, who lived at home with him, and a girl, who lived with her mother. He had divorced three years ago, and by the tone of his voice when he spoke of old times and about his ex-wife, it was obvious that he was still mourning for the life that they had had together.

She looked at his profile and bit her lip. It was the first time that a man other than Jules aroused in her an instantaneous interest. Sebastian's arms had wrapped her body so tenderly when they danced...

"This is my house," Sebastian said, as he pulled into his driveway, unaware of her remembrance.

Sebastian's house was not very large, but comfortable and in order.

"Joel, Al, Kris, where are you?" he called as he pulled open the back door and stepped in. He turned to Alexandra. "Come in. Make yourself at home." As he said that, Sebastian's sons came running into the kitchen. "These are my children," Sebastian said proudly brushing one of his son's heads.

Alexandra bit her lip, she was nervous. Sebastian's sons were standing one beside the other, looking at her with suspicion.

It is normal. Alexandra thought. If my father had brought a woman in our house after my mother died, I would have acted the same way. "Hi," she said in loud voice, trying to be friendly as Sebastian pulled her by the hand, and took her into his bedroom.

Sebastian's bedroom was clean, and the arrangement inviting. It was so easy to kiss him. She wanted him more than anything at that moment, and he seemed so incredibly gentle and attractive.

She felt an uncontrollable tremor. Sebastian's sweet hands were rolling along her back up and down with warm tenderness.

86

After work there was always this rush in her heart to meet with Sebastian, for six months she loved him madly, and that's how it happened--she was pregnant. Tonight, she was going to give him the news. Her little son, Franco was in the bedroom, asleep. She kissed him in the forehead softly and walked around the room impatiently. Sebastian always came around eleven o'clock to see her, stayed with her for a couple of hours then, he left. Right now it was ten past eleven. The bell's ringing caused her heart to beat vigorously. She was so in love with Sebastian. His sole remembrance incited emotions that she never felt. She opened the door anxiously, and Sebastian walked up the stairs slowly. His shirt was opened half way, showing his virile chest. His brown, silky hair kinked freely about his forehead.

There was no light in the living room, only the moonlight filtering through the blinds. It didn't matter. Alexandra knew Sebastian's features one by one. Her hands had caressed many times his skin, delineating every corner of his body, adoring every little bit of him...

They sat on the carpet one in front of the other. She had no furniture and no money--the living room was bare. In one corner over a brick, a small vase of daisies stood still. In the small kitchen were an old table and a chair. In the bedroom was a mattress on the floor where her son lay asleep, some books on a shelf, and a small television over a stool. Everything was clean.

"Sebastian," Alexandra said, "I'm pregnant." She breathed deeply trying to disguise the tremor of her voice and looking straight at Sebastian.

Sebastian's fists closed. She couldn't see him well, but she sensed that there was trouble in his face.

"I love you. I want to marry you," she continued tremulously, ignoring his rigid posture.

"I could never marry someone who has a black son," said Sebastian dryly as he rose to his feet. "To think of that possibility would be like the dreamer without fingers that wants to become a pianist. It would never happen." He walked about the room. "I don't love you. I never have." His voice was icy. "I am seeing someone else. She is from Idaho. I have many things in common with her, with you I don't have any." He paused. "I will cover the cost for the abortion." He moved one hand to reach his pocket.

Alexandra's eyes closed momentarily. She tried to say something, but she couldn't. The words had dried inside her mouth like the dead leaves of autumn. The room seemed to be twirling around her, and her soul shivered. His words were still hammering her head in cruel agony. Alexandra stood up and moved back. Her tears had dripped over his body many times in ecstacy, but tonight, nothing about him was manly. He had turned into a coward that wanted to get away from it all.

Sebastian walked towards her. "Alexandra--" he muttered.

"I asked you a question and you gave me an answer. We have nothing else to say. You can leave now." Alexandra said with icy calm.

Sebastian stared at her with surprise. He stood still for a second, disconcerted, then, he walked again towards her.

"Leave," Alexandra demanded.

Suddenly Sebastian raised his hands to his head. "My head!" he cried sorrowfully bumping his head on the wall repeatedly. Something like a crazed look gleamed his eyes.

"Leave," Alexandra repeated coldly ignoring his sudden outburst. "Go back to the only people you care for--your family."

Still lamenting about his headache, Sebastian climbed the stairs without turning once to see her, and went out.

The sound of Sebastian's steps fading into the night filled Alexandra's ears. She stayed shocked for a moment, then, she fell on the floor, trying in vain to quiet her cries. What Sebastian told her about her son, hurt her more than telling her that he had never loved her, but what else could she have expected from a man for whom his own baby didn't matter and who had offered to pay for an abortion? It was beyond belief. His reaction was like a crazy nightmare that she was witnessing through a distorted mirror.

87

Since the night Alexandra told Sebastian she was pregnant, Sebastian hadn't come back—he didn't care, he said so. That's why she was parked in front of his house waiting. She wanted to talk things over with him; he couldn't be so insensitive. Alexandra's heart leaped as Sebastian's car pulled into his driveway. A short, scarlet-headed woman got out of his car laughing. As Sebastian helped her out, he pulled her firmly towards him. Holding one another, they walked to the back door and went into the house lovingly, unaware of her presence.

Alexandra got out of her car and walked rapidly towards Sebastian's house. The back door was opened, and she went in, crossing the kitchen and going directly to the living room. Her heart was pounding furiously. She tried to breath deeply but a choking sensation seemed to possess her. Her eyes met Sebastian's in quiet protest. The short, scarlet-headed woman was sitting in front of the organ, playing and smiling, while Sebastian stood near her, watching.

"I saw the door open, and I came in", Alexandra's said, her voice cracking.

The woman glanced at her quickly, then, continued playing the organ.

Sebastian came towards Alexandra promptly as he kept looking with apprehension at the woman who continued playing, oblivious to the surroundings.

"This is Mary, my lady friend," Sebastian hurried to say.

The woman stopped playing the organ, turned her head and looked at Alexandra.

"This is Alexandra, a neighbor," explained Sebastian to the woman without traces of guilt on his face.

The woman said "Hi," then, turned and resumed playing the organ.

229

Alexandra's eyes were fixed on Sebastian's as if a strange force had glued them to his. She was five months pregnant, she had a sharp pain inside and a tremendous desire to scream, but she couldn't.

Unable to cope with Alexandra's presence and the reproach in her face, Sebastian passed by her and disappeared in the kitchen. For a moment Alexandra stared at Mary attentively. The woman's eyes resembled the eyes of an eagle--icy, glass-like, and piercing. She moved slowly, like a serpent, calculating every movement. Looking at her, it was easy to see that Mary knew exactly where she was, what she wanted, and how to get it.

Alexandra had seen enough. The woman was obviously secure of her charm--she wasn't, Sebastian had shattered her dreams, he had dumped her and his baby without regrets. Alexandra walked slowly towards the front door and went out.

88

The remaining months of her pregnancy Sebastian dated alternatively Mary and a Chinese woman. Alexandra had seen them on and off with him through his window. It was sickening to realize the way he shared his sexuality so freely, and so absurd for her to still have feelings towards him despite the way he fooled her and insulted her.

"Let's go, mommy" the voice of her little son pulled her back from Sebastian's window and from her thoughts.

She kissed her son tenderly. He was all her life. He and only he had illuminated her path with his innocent and trustful smile, and with the beauty of his soul. The only true loves she had were her son, and the baby on the way. She needed to endure for them, to provide for them, and to protect them from the injustice that sometimes was so difficult to avoid in life.

She held her son's hand and ran with him back home, struggling not to let her tears fall. The night smelled like jasmine. "It is so comfortable being with you," was all Sebastian ever told her, and she had fallen for that. She had been a fool, but when she met Sebastian, she felt alive again. The sun seemed to illuminate the world all of a sudden with good and beauty. Jules circumspect, cold, and absent eyes at the side of Sebastian were fading and erasing the grief he had caused her, and Warren, he was married, he was a love that was never meant to be.

89

She was at work when the labor started. She had gone to the bathroom, and there the blood ran between her legs, falling like a shower to the floor. An intense panic overpowered her. She was scared to move and embarrassed to walk out of the bathroom bleeding. No one else was in the restroom. She wiped the blood that had fallen on the toilet and on the floor with big masses of toilet paper, washed her hands, splashed her face with cold water where pearls of sweat were forming, and, moving very slowly, walked towards the hallway.

A man who worked in a nearby office passed by her.

"Could you tell the in-charge that I can't continue working? I am bleeding in labor. My name is Alexandra."

The guy looked at her as if she were crazy. Turning pale, he rushed towards the office where she worked to spread the news. As she waited for the guy to come back, her heart was pounding madly. What was she going to do now? Her little son was at school. She had to let him know somehow that she wasn't coming home that evening. The hospital where she was going to deliver was 12 blocks away from work, and she didn't have a car. She caught the bus everyday.

She worked downtown, in one of the oldest buildings in the city. She got the job passing the required tests and by writing on the application that she was a citizen. She had fair skin and she was blond, so there hadn't been many questions.

Her supervisor looked appalled. She was a thin, elderly woman of sweet and gentle countenance; her small and smiling blue eyes were almost lost behind her spectacles.

"I'll take you to the hospital," she said. "My car is two blocks away from here. I can walk to get the car and come back here to get you."

"I'll walk with you. I am too nervous to wait here," Alexandra said.

"Will you be all right walking?"

"I think so," Alexandra replied, but she didn't know. She was alone and scared, and did not want to wait.

Her supervisor walked with her to the parking lot and drove her to the main hospital entrance. There, Alexandra got out.

"Thank you," she told her supervisor.

"Do you want me to notify your husband?" she questioned.

I don't have a husband," Alexandra said, looking away. "I'll be all right. Don't worry. Thanks again."

Her supervisor looked at her with disbelief, said "good luck," and pulled away.

Alexandra walked to the front desk and checked into the hospital.

90

After Alexandra checked into the hospital, she called her neighbor.

"Louise? This is Alexandra calling. I am in the hospital in labor. I have no way to notify my son. Can you go to my home to let him and to take him to the Bishop's house? He must be back from school by now. Can you do that for me, please?"

"Of course I'll do that." Alexandra heard the surprised voice of Louise. "Do you want me to notify Sebastian? After all, it's his baby. He should be there with you."

Louise was the only one who knew about Sebastian.

"No!" Alexandra shouted. "Please don't. Just go to my son and take him to the Bishop's house."

"All right, as you like."

"Thank you," Alexandra said with relief, and hung up.

The last time she had seen Sebastian had been two months ago, when she had the nonsense to go see him at work in the hopes of touching his paternal side. It was lunchtime, and for that reason she found him alone in his office.

"Don't come here again!" he warned, enraged, throwing his arms into the air, "I don't want to see you here, or crawling around my house. If you do, I will put a bullet through my head right in front of you! I don't love you. You and I have nothing in common, don't you understand?" His face had flushed, his eyes were piercing, and his mouth was unleashed. "What are you doing here?" he ranted on. "Why don't you move?" He paced from one side of the office to the other. "You always went from place to place. Why did you have to fall here like a satellite, where I've lived in tranquility all my life? He stopped his pacing and looked at her with hate. "The devil must have sent you to destroy me!" he added as he sat down, covering his eyes with his hands as though to avoid the horrifying view he had in front of him.

Alexandra, offended and crushed, hadn't moved from the door. She was trying to remember where she had heard words like those before. Slowly, without having said a word she turned on her steps and left.

91

Her little baby girl came to the world after twelve hours of struggle. It was three twenty six in the morning when the melodious cry invaded her soul.

"It's a little girl!" the doctor and the nurse shouted joyously.

"Let me see her," Alexandra murmured, raising her chest from the delivery table.

She had seen everything through the ceiling mirror, but having her baby near was an incomparable feeling. The nurse took her baby over to the nearest sink, washed her, and when she had dressed her, she brought her back again.

"Well, what do you think of this?" The nurse was smiling.

Alexandra looked at her little bundle with admiration and tenderness; mute tears of love fell freely from her eyes.

"Do you want to hold her?" the nurse asked.

"Yes please, yes."

The nurse left Alexandra's baby on Alexandra's stomach and went away, allowing her to savor the gratifying feelings. She was a lovely baby! The tiny piece of heaven that she had been waiting for with such longing and love was here at last. Her emerald eyes were wide open, looking attentively at her and smiling. She was so little, pretty, and perfect.

92

"You can give your child up for adoption," her Bishop said, businesslike.

He had come to the hospital to see her, and after congratulating her politely for her new baby he couldn't wait to offer "his help".

"It is very hard to raise a child as a single mother," he continued, "and you already have one. You have a job, but as high as the inflation is, you won't be able to manage. It is too much responsibility. If you want, I can arrange an appointment with a social worker as soon as you get out of the hospital to give up your child for adoption."

"Bishop," she said coldly, "I am not planning to give my child up for adoption. I am in a hard situation, but I am capable of doing whatever it takes for my children. Children aren't things that you just give away to avoid the burden and the responsibility. Would you give up yours? I love my children. Don't you love yours?"

What a nerve! She thought after he was gone. This was the very reason that she preferred to be alone: to avoid hearing the absurd decisions that others made about her life due to the predicament of her condition.

93

It was snowing when they checked out of the hospital. The tiny snowflakes shone like diamonds in the light of the spring sun as the birds sang cheerfully. She had her soul in her arms where her little baby girl slept peacefully, ignorant of the magnificent world around her. Alexandra stepped out with determination, looking upward to the sky. She was ready to fight; God was giving her the opportunity of the best glory someone could ever have. She had two children! Whatever she did would affect them. She wanted to be a pillar of strength on which her little ones could always lean when they needed it.

She set her tiny baby in the crib and held her little son, who had been watching all of her movements with those loving and sweet black eyes of his. She kissed him over and over, holding him tight as she showed him his baby sister.

"You and her, my little one," she told him, "are the most important persons in my life, did you know that?"

Her little boy nodded and kissed her back. Until now he had been her only companion. He had been with her through loneliness, rejection, suffering, cries, insults, and joys. He was a fighter, a miracle of strength, fortitude, and goodwill. Looking at him together with his little sister, the tenderness she felt inside was incredible. Her little boy's eyes were glowing with that light that was the lucid reflection of his soul.

Suddenly, the doorbell rang. She stood up and looked through the window. It was Sebastian. He was carrying his film equipment, and she assumed he was there to take some pictures of his daughter. Her neighbor, ignoring her request not to notify Sebastian, had called him to let him know that his little daughter was born, but Sebastian, overlooking Louise's news, didn't go to the hospital to meet his baby. Alexandra shook those thoughts out of her mind and opened the door, hiding her tremor.

"Hi," he said, passing through. "Where is she?"

When he came, he never said hello to her little son. She bit her lips.

"In the bedroom," she added.

He walked towards the bedroom and Alexandra and her son followed him. Her little son was smiling happily. He was excited that Sebastian was going to meet his little sister.

Alexandra's little baby was sleeping on a bright red quilt on the bed. She was three days old, and she was absolutely precious. With her eyes closed, she looked like an angel. Alexandra picked her up carefully, and said, "Carly, this is your daddy."

"She is beautiful!" Sebastian said, as he stared at Carly for a minute open-mouthed. Then he turned about, grabbed his camera, and began to take picture after picture.

"Would you like to hold her?" Alexandra asked, when he finished the roll of film.

Sebastian extended his arms and took the baby from her arms. He held high, as he observed her attentively, and then down, high and then down on the bed.

"She is the most beautiful baby I've ever seen," he said, as he closed his camera and put it back in its case. "How old is she?" he asked.

"Three days old."

"Well, I'd better be going."

A second later he was gone, back to his life and away from them.

She had maternity leave for six weeks. She was lucky--to be with her children was all she wanted. At home, she was free from the inquiring looks of people and their questions. She had come to Utah with the idea of finding the perfect place to live, but what she found was nothing but disappointment.

94

The sound of the bell took her away from her reading. It was Sebastian. It had been a month since he came to take the baby's pictures.

"I brought the pictures I've taken of your little daughter," he said, stepping in.

Then he held her, and Alexandra fell in his arms. She had this love for him. Apologies and words weren't necessary when he was with her surrendering in bliss to her soul, to her mind, and to her body. Sebastian stayed for an hour, then, he crept on tiptoe and walked out the door. Alexandra rose right after him with an uneasy feeling and got dressed. Quietly, she went into the bedroom where her children were asleep, and when she made sure they were fine she went into the street, closing the door after her. The street at midnight was in complete stillness and her heart was beating so loudly that it frightened her. Containing her fright and the anxious beating of her heart, she ran all the way to Sebastian's house. He lived two blocks away and within minutes she reached his house. Sebastian's house was fully illuminated. The chinese woman's car that she had seen many times parked on the street in front of Sebastian's house was there. Alexandra felt a sudden dread. The front window curtains were opened. Coming closer she peeped inside and froze; inside, the Chinese woman and Sebastian were kissing. He was caressing her madly, as if he were hungry for her touch and his only reason for existence was being with her at that moment.

For a few seconds, Alexandra stayed paralyzed trying to make sense of the objectionable behavior. Sebastian's love was treason. It didn't last much, only the brief second that he had come to fool her. She left the window and ran back home crazily as bitter tears sprang out of her eyes in humiliation and pain. At home, her little children were still asleep. She leaned quietly over them and kissed them with devotion. Then she went in silence to the living room where she had just been in Sebastian's arms and, falling on her knees, she cried till she had no tears.

"If he comes again," she said. "I won't open the door."

But he didn't come the next day or the next. Two weeks later Sebastian showed up at Alexandra's house again.

What does he want? Alexandra wondered when she saw him. She was firmly resolved not to open the door, but looking at him from behind the window awakened uncontrollable feelings, a burning humiliation, an inexplicable love, hate, revolt, and overall, an overwhelming sorrow. Crying, she fell into his arms.

How could I love such a loathsome man? She pondered as she washed his body with her tears.

95

Alexandra approached Sebastian's house quickly and went in.

She hadn't seen him for four weeks. He had made it a routine to take her at his pleasure and then, dumped her just like trash. She closed the door behind her and Alexandra came face to face with the Chinese woman. She was standing in the middle of the kitchen with a glass in her hand.

"Hi," Alexandra said. "Is Sebastian home?"

The woman looked at her in amazement. "Why? Who are you?"

"My name is Alexandra. Sebastian and I have a baby. She is three months old."

"You have a baby from him? I don't believe it." She exclaimed in surprise.

"You don't need to believe it." Alexandra answered. "Sebastian is going with you, with me, and a woman who spends the nights with him when you don't spend the night with him. He is toying with everyone's feelings."

"I want to see your baby. Where do you live?"

"I live on 2051 South. 2100 East." Alexandra said. " It's apartment 9."

"I'll be there in fifteen or thirty minutes," the Chinese woman said. "I'm waiting for Sebastian."

"That's fine." Alexandra said and stepped out without further delay.

She didn't know why she had done it, but it was done. Sebastian's scheme was on the light, at least before the eyes of this Chinese woman. Sebastian had a baby with her and he did not care. He behaved recklessly, not minding the pain and the destruction that he was leaving in his wake.

"Thanks, my little darling," Alexandra said to her son, who had stayed taking care of his little sister while she went to Sebastian's. "You can go to your football practice now."

"O.K. mommy."

Franco was now eight years old. The school where he attended and practiced football in the evenings was located a few yards away from the apartments. The apartment complex was not the best, but that was all they needed. She had the convenience of the school close by, the laundry a block away, the grocery store two blocks further, and the bus stop one block away.

Alexandra paced about the room wondering what would happen next. By now, the Chinese woman had probably confronted Sebastian with his deceit. She thought. At that moment the bell rang, interrupting her thoughts.

"I am going to kill you!" Sebastian stepped in as soon as she opened the door, smacking the door and then the walls with his fists. "Who gave you the right to tell Miko about us, damn woman!" he yelled and puffed as his eyes gleamed with anger and his jaw was clenched. "I hate you! I've never told you I love you! Why did you have to interfere in my life? You little damn fucking son of a bitchen snake."

He was still swearing when the bell rang again.

"Are you there, Sebastian?" the Chinese woman called in a loud voice from downstairs.

"It's her!" Sebastian cried, turning pale. "Tell her I am not here!" he exclaimed with anxiety, as he rushed into the bathroom, then cautiously went to hide behind the bathtub curtain.

Hardly believing what she had just witnessed and heard, Alexandra went downstairs and opened the door.

"Where is he?" The Chinese woman yelled, angrily.

"Upstairs," Alexandra said, feeling a sudden weakness.

"Where?" The Chinese woman asked, not seeing him around.

"There." Alexandra pointed in the direction of the bathroom behind the curtain.

"What are you doing here? You little son of a bitch; coward!" she bullied him as she pulled away the curtain and surprised Sebastian.

"You didn't want me to find you huh? You didn't know her huh? Then, what are you doing here?" The Chinese woman screamed grinding her teeth as Sebastian crept from behind the curtain like a chastised dog.

He had lost his fury. His features had softened, and in the woman's presence, Sebastian seemed apologetic and inhibited.

This cannot be happening, Alexandra thought, incredulous.

Carly, awakened with the screams, was crying loudly. Alexandra went into the bedroom and held her tenderly in her arms. "Hush, my baby, hush," she said. "Everything will be all right."

With the baby in her arms, she went back to the living room and stood still in the corner near the kitchen door. In the middle of the living room Sebastian was now holding the woman.

"Forgive me!" he begged her, while abundant tears dropped from his eyes. "I love you. Don't treat me this way! I love you!" He looked pitiful.

"Don't touch me, you pig!" the woman demanded with a powerful, voice as she hit him with her fists, trying to push him away from her. "You love me, so what are you doing here with her? While you were with me, you and she made a baby." She pointed at Alexandra and the baby.

"She is lying. That is not my baby!" he mourned pitifully. "I love you!"

"She said that she is," The Chinese woman persisted.

"She is not. She is not my baby, she is lying!" Sebastian insisted, "and if she is, I don't want her. She means nothing to me."

"If your baby means nothing to you, then what does?" Miko shouted even louder than before as she continued to punch his chest.

Sebastian glanced at Alexandra, his face contorted in anger.

"I hate you, I hate you!" He said in rage. "Why did you have to tell her? I never told you I love you! I hate you! Miko is the only woman I ever loved and I am going to marry her!" His eyes were filled with hatred, and the tone of his voice had changed from supplication to accusation. "Tell her I never told you I love you--tell her!" He demanded.

Alexandra looked at him disconcertedly.

Well, she thought, why don't they go, and leave me alone? She had seen and heard more than she wanted.

"Shut up!" the Chinese woman screamed, this time pushing him back with both arms, hitting his chest with fury. "You love me, but you can't have me! I'm married and you know it!"

So, Alexandra thought, staring at them attentively, this is the only woman that he ever loved, an adulterous deceiver just like he is.

"If Miko leaves me," Sebastian said, turning threateningly to Alexandra and wringing his hands, "I am going to kill you!"

Alexandra's body quivered. Sebastian wasn't lying, she knew. There was too much hate and aggression in his voice for that.

"If you do anything to her," the Chinese woman hissed, shaking her fists in the air, "I'll take care of you--you know I will." Her voice grew louder.

The expression on Sebastian's face changed abruptly. He muttered softly as more tears ran silently from his eyes, "I love you, I love you."

The sword had hit its target. It was more than Alexandra could possibly bear.

"Go!" Alexandra demanded, lifting her eyes. "Leave! Whatever else you two want to discuss, please discuss it outside. I don't want any more screams in here. You are scaring my baby." Alexandra paused, gasping for breath. "As for you, Sebastian, you don't have to come to kill me. I told her about us because I thought that you loved me, and that your baby meant something to you." She paused, looking around in dismay. "Now I know that I was wrong--we don't mean anything to you. You just said it. If I had known you loved Miko that much, I wouldn't have interfered in your relationship and caused you so much unhappiness. I am sorry I did, I hope she doesn't leave you so you can be happy." When she finished, she was quivering, frightened of his hate.

"Let's get out of here," Miko commanded, heading out and pulling Sebastian by the hand.

As a dog following his master, Sebastian turned and went after the Chinese woman, temperate and submissive, wiping the last tears from his eyes.

It was fortunate that Franco wasn't here, she reflected as she saw them leave. It would have been a terrifying experience for him, as it had been for her. She moved around the apartment nervously. She wanted to close her brain to the remembrance, but Sebastian's words still sounded in her ears loud and clear. He said he was going to kill her and she was scared. Passionate crimes were committed many times for less significant reasons than that, and Sebastian seemed lustily in love with Miko: a married woman.

96

At night Alexandra saw Sebastian come. She had just barely got up to feed her baby when she looked warily through the window as if she had known, and then her heart stopped. He was coming across the street despite the copious rain, arguing with his two oldest sons, who seemed to be trying to persuade him to go back. A thick belt around his chest supported the rifle that he held in his hands as he walked decisively toward Alexandra's place.

She stepped aside from the window, climbed on the kitchen counter, and peeked out from behind the kitchen curtain, almost afraid to breath. Everything was silent and dark except the loud and unintelligible voices that came from outside and the intermittent drops of rain that hit the windowpane.

Carly began to cry with hunger, startling Alexandra for a moment. She left the window and crawled on the floor to get the milk, and then, kneeling down, she warmed it on the stove. Her body was shaking. Sebastian hadn't lied. He had come to kill her. It didn't matter that she was the mother of his child, or that Franco and his baby would become orphans.

"If only I wouldn't have gone?" She mourned. She felt a profound guilt and regret over letting her feelings dominate her reason. It was because of her carelessness and insensitivity that she had put her kids in danger and herself in this predicament.

After feeding the baby, she tucked Carly in the cradle, and crawling again, afraid to be seen from the window, she came back to the kitchen and peeped outside. Sebastian was now with his two sons under the pine tree that grew a few yards in front of her window. She could see them perfectly in the glare of the dim street lamp, which also shone on the golden part of the rifle.

"What is he waiting for?" She whispered in despair. "He is probably waiting for me to come to the kitchen, and as I turn the light on he will shoot me."

The rain hadn't stopped and it was obvious that by now Sebastian and his sons must have been soaking wet.

Waiting was causing her tension to grow to an almost unbearable point. For two hours she watched them through the edge of the window, weary. They didn't come out from under the tree, and they did not move. At 4 o'clock in the morning, they left. Apparently his sons had finally convinced him to desist. Alexandra left the window feeling weak. Her mouth was dry and her heart was hammering painfully.

"Thank God I am safe for now, but tomorrow..."

She fell on her bed, exhausted, and covered her cold and shivering body with the blanket. She closed her eyes. She was spinning in a roller coaster, falling at high speed, then, she floated until she came to a stand still...

97

She went back to work that Monday. Her maternity leave had ended. Things had to return to the routine they had always been except that now she had another baby. Nothing was more painful for her than leaving her baby in the hands of a stranger and seeing the distress her absence caused in her little boy, but she needed to work to make a living. Ignoring her pain, she left her baby with the baby sitter then, she walked her little boy to school.

"I'll be home two hours after you get home from school. Your little sister will be with the baby sitter in apartment 14 until I get back. You have the house key in your pocket and I left a sandwich in the refrigerator if you are hungry. Don't open the door to anybody while I'm gone."

" O.K, mommy," Franco said. "I love you."

"I love you, too."

They kissed, and her son leaving her arms, ran across the school field.

"Bye." She shouted.

Her son turned his head and waved. Her heart was aching. She shut out the oppressive thoughts, and walking straight and determinedly, she went to the bus stop. As a single parent, even though her heart was left with her children, she needed to put up a shield to her problems in order to function as a normal breadwinner in the real world. At work she was somebody else. She feigned to have no troubles and forced herself to smile.

"Hi Alexandra," everyone greeted happily.

"How is your baby?" one asked.

"Fine," she answered briskly, walking faster and looking down.

She feared their questions. People's questions always forced her to lie. It was preferable to be judged unfriendly, than to repeat time after time that she was divorced and the rest of the lies she had fabricated to protect her illegal status in the country and her private life.

"Franco! Mommy is home, darling." She came into her apartment running, hoping to find him well.

Franco was watching television in the bedroom. He lifted his eyes and the biggest smile crossed his face.

"Mommy, it's so good to see you."

Alexandra came anxiously towards him and hugged him and kissed him.

"Come," she said, half-calm now. "Let's go get your little sister."

Hand in hand, they walked rapidly to apartment fourteen. Her heart was pounding. She wouldn't be in absolute peace until her little baby girl was again in her arms and she made sure that both of her kids were well, just as she had left them.

The baby sitter opened the door, and with a trembling voice, Alexandra asked. "How is she? Is she all right? Did she eat well? Did she cry?"

"She is fine, don't worry." The baby-sitter laughed. "There she is." She pointed at the couch where Carly was asleep.

Alexandra held her baby in her arms tenderly, breathing, at last, totally at peace. She had found both of her kids fine thank God.

98

"Alexandra, will you come to my office for a second?"

Alexandra turned her head. It was Mrs. Ross. She was the in charged at work that evening.

"Sure." She said, as she stood up, then, proceeded to follow Mrs. Ross into her office.

"Do you have any enemies?" Mrs. Ross said, looking right into Alexandra's eyes.

"None that I know of," she said cautiously not knowing the reason for that question. "Why?"

"Do you know a Sebastian Makowski?"

Alexandra assented.

"Is he your friend?" Mrs. Ross asked.

"He is the father of my baby."

Mrs. Ross played with the pencil she had in her hands, nervously. "He called yesterday night to say that you are an illegal alien. Do you know why he said that?"

Alexandra knew that the color must have left her face.

"No." she answered briefly, feeling a sinking feeling in the pit of the stomach.

Mrs. Ross looked at her straight in the eye, "I think he wants to harm you. Be careful." She said.

Sebastian was capable of anything. Even to generously exposing her as he had, to be fired and to be deported. Alexandra gave Mrs. Ross a stared look--she was black, in her mid-sixties. She would be retiring soon. Alexandra liked her. Mrs. Ross had the reputation of being understanding and kind. Alexandra bit her lip nervously. It was obvious that Mrs. Ross had figured out the truth. The question was-- was she going to turn her in? I have to be calm, I need the job, she thought.

"I had no idea that this happened. I will be careful."

"I just wanted to warn you. He can be dangerous."

"Yes," Alexandra answered quickly not wanting to make a big issue of the incident. "Thanks for letting me know."

Trembling she went back to work. She worked like crazy the rest of the day. At the end of the day, she went to Sebastian's office. It was a little past five thirty, just in time before closing. In three strides she crossed the reception area, pushed the door and walked into his office.

"How dare you, calling my job to expose me." Alexandra recriminated. "Only someone with no scruples and filled with evil can concoct something like that. If they fire me, you have something to be proud of for the rest of your life."

Sebastian who was sitting behind his desk, as she came in stood up turning purple. "I don't know why you hate me," Alexandra continued, "I gave you my trust and you betrayed me, I gave you my love and you stepped on me, I bared your child and you don't care. If you don't help me, don't harm me. It is not only me who will go down. If I go down, my kids go down with me. I just came to thank you for what you have done for me and my kids. It's incredible!" The tears were springing down her cheeks. She didn't wait for an answer, she walked out of there as if she were followed by a thousand demons and cried all the way home.

99

Alexandra woke up at the sound of the doorbell. She rubbed her eyes in alarm and looked at the clock. It was 2.30 a.m.

It can't be! She thought, getting up and looking at Sebastian through the window.

"What do you want?" she asked dryly from the window. "Are you coming to kill me?"

"Open up," Sebastian commanded, looking away.

"I am not going to open the door," Alexandra affirmed.

"You don't love me, don't you remember?" she added sardonically. "You said so the last time you were here. Your little daughter is not yours. You call my work to get rid of me last night. Have you forgotten?"

"Open up," he insisted stubbornly.

"What for?" she asked with disdain. "To entertain you for a little while and then have you take me to immigration?"

"Come down and open the door. I want to talk to you."

"You want to talk, but I don't. I want you to leave before you wake up the neighbors."

"I won't leave until I talk to you," he shouted while ringing the doorbell intermittently.

"Please! Be quiet," she implored, apprehensively. "This is not my house, I'm renting."

The loud tone of his voice was an effective strategy, because Alexandra, fearing that the neighbors would call the police, and that their presence would lead to her deportation—came down to open the door.

Sebastian didn't have to come too close to her to know that he was drunk. The odor coming from his body was strong and his eyes had a glazed look. Now what? Alexandra thought in irritation. "What did you want to tell me?" she asked coldly.

Sebastian extended his arms and drew her towards him, looking at her in the eye supplicant.

"Oh no, not again. Go! You can't stay!" she jumped backwards like a hurt cat, knowing that as soon as she made the mistake of succumbing to his arms and forget all grievances, he would turn around to fall in the arms of Miko.

But Sebastian didn't move.

"Sebastian, I want you to leave. Don't you understand? You have toyed with me, insulted me enough and even attempted to put my job in jeopardy. I don't want to talk to you today. We'll talk tomorrow." She pushed him softly towards the door, then firmly until she closed the door behind him.

She went upstairs and sat on the couch, relieved, closing her eyes.

100

It was a matter of pure chance, otherwise how could Alexandra explain meeting Sebastian at the store the next day holding hands with Miko. She stopped in her tracks to observe them. Sebastian looked bewildered. At that instant, he stopped in his steps to kiss Miko and to babble something in her ear that caused her to wiggle. Even at a distance, Alexandra could distinctly see how his chest heaved with emotion, and how secure Miko felt in the control she exercised over him. Tall and thin, Miko moved at Sebastian's side agilely, like an artful warrior. A few steps behind them, was Sebastian's mother, pacing with arrogance down the aisle. A half smile was on her haughty face as she walked forward, moving her head like a peacock, evidently proud to be shopping at the side of her son and her daughter-in-law.

"How ungracefully humorous!" Alexandra said to herself. "Sebastian has introduced an adulterous woman as his fiancée to his mother, but he did not want to introduce me."

"That would never happen," Sebastian had told her many times. "We are a traditional white middle class family; we would never accept a black in our midst."

He had enunciated this with exceeding vanity, proud of the distinguished and privileged status that he had in society just by reason of the color of his skin. It had been a major insult to her, but, she corrected herself--there had been even greater insults that he had come out with. There were the barbaric cruelties he had said about her son Franco, and about his little daughter, when he affirmed that she wasn't his.

Alexandra walked towards them with the intention that Sebastian could see her. Just when she was at a short distance from them, she stopped. At this moment Sebastian turned and their eyes met. Like a robber caught in the act, Sebastian turned pale, and Alexandra looked straight into his face with pity, as if she were scrutinizing his soul for all those things that he did that were objectionable and unspeakable. In an instant, the half jolly smile that was on Sebastian's mother's face disappeared, replaced by a frown of indignation. A devilish shock distorted Miko's enamored face.

"Get out of here, you damn fucking bitch!" Sebastian's mother screamed, moving three steps forward with her hands up in the air, shaking with fury. "Leave my son alone and take your nigger and your bastard illegitimate baby away from us! We don't want them! Sebastian will never marry you, you hear? Go! Get out!"

Alexandra blushed and drew back slowly. She was still staring at Sebastian and Miko with an eager, almost maniacal look as they walked confused and nervous in the aisles. Alexandra continued to walk back to the exit door, ignoring Sebastian's mother's looks that still eyed her with profound disgust and hatred. She reached the door and began to run home. Her nerves were overstrained. The more she analyzed the circumstances, the more she realized that Miko and Sebastian seemed to be made for each other. They both had no scruples and seemed to possess the same goal: to gratify their lowest and most hideous wants regardless of whom they stepped on.

101

That night Sebastian came to her house, like a shameless person would come, without a pinch of regret, as if what he had done was a stroke of grace and she had to greet him and applaud him. Alexandra covered her face with her hands in desperation and looked at him incredulously. She had vowed to herself not to open the door, nevertheless, at his presence, judgments, turned to silence and submission. As though hypnotized, she opened the door shamefully. Her thoughts ran in a frenzy agitated by her own weakness. She felt miserable. Sebastian made her love degrading and obscure, instead of simple, clear, open, and dignified.

When she opened the door, Sebastian's eyes flashed egotistically, secure in his knowledge that he had her in his hands once more. Alexandra felt like screaming and crying at the same time, tortured by his presence and his malice. With him she had descended to the very depths of hell... and for that she hated him with all the power of her being.

"You are a degenerate!" she accused crying and falling in his arms.

"If you get upset with what I do, I am not responsible," he said, shrugging his shoulders indifferently. "Everyone is responsible for what they allow themselves to feel."

102

Three days passed by without a sight of Sebastian or a phone call. He was behaving no different than he always had, but she was a war of nerves and she couldn't help it. Dealing with Sebastian was like being in action waiting for an attack not ever knowing where the bullets would come from. She had been watching television to distract her thoughts for about an hour, when all of a sudden she had a strange hunch. That's why she was outside Sebastian's house waiting in her car for his arrival. She hadn't been parked there more than two minutes, when Sebastian pulled into his driveway. He wasn't alone--the woman with him was Mary.

Lacing her by the waist, they headed towards the back door.

Alexandra got out of her car and with quick strides she followed them. She wasn't surprised. Sebastian was living as always what he considered life at its best—tasting small bites of the gourmet that he had available on the table.

"Great!" Sebastian exclaimed when he saw her. He pulled the woman by the hand and hurried to enter his house just in time to slam the door in Alexandra's face.

"Open the door, Sebastian!" Alexandra yelled as she banged on the door. "Tell this woman that you are a crook! Tell her that you have a little baby girl with me, and that when she doesn't come to spend the night with you, you take turns with Miko. Tell her!"

"Who is this woman?" Alexandra heard Mary ask Sebastian with acute indignation while she continued to bang the door.

"It's a crazy woman who lives in the neighborhood. She thinks she has a baby from me," Sebastian explained. "Let's just ignore her. She always knocks at my door, and when she gets tired--she leaves," Sebastian concluded this statement laughing and pulling the woman by the hand into the other room.

Alexandra banged the door harder as loud music, coming from inside the house, obliterated her knocks, and her screams.
"Coward! You coward!"

103

"What we feel for each other is strong. Nothing can destroy the bond that exists between us. I love you. What I feel with you, I feel with no one." He said.

Alexandra had Sebastian in front of her. The night before he had just betrayed her, and now again he had the nerve to come. Well, it was not that she believed him--Carly loved him. Sebastian's words, now that the thrill was gone, for her were just like chatter.

Of course, she had the idea of the Cinderella dream, the once in a lifetime love, but after eight years of waiting for a committed relationship, Sebastian got all wrong--when things were tough, when she needed him for something, he skipped his visits for a few months pretending to be upset, or he simply detached himself as if he felt no part of them and their problems. Alexandra moved aside to let him in. "I need to talk to you." She said.

Sebastian stepped in and went to sit down in the sofa.

"It's a nice day isn't it?"

"Sebastian, I need your help to fix my immigration papers. Without them, my situation in this country is very unstable." She paused to glance at him. "I can't live in peace when I'm constantly fearing, that someone will finally figure out my status in this country, and that I end up being deported. Can you help me?"

A hard veil fell immediately over Sebastian's eyes, turning them opaque.

"You had those problems before I met you," he said insolently, closing his fists. "I am not going to be the one to solve them for you."

Alexandra bit her lip. She knew that what he felt for her wasn't love. She diverted her eyes to conceal her disappointment. He didn't know how suddenly gruesome, and how intensely unloving he had turned again before her eyes.

Sebastian stood up and walked with arrogance to the refrigerator, got a soda pop, and drank it. He was so accustomed to his impudent manners that he didn't even have the tact to know that his attitude was out of the ordinary.

Despite her thoughts, Alexandra had nothing else to say. His aloof response was a reminder of where she and her children stood in his eyes. All that mattered to Sebastian was to safeguard his autonomy and his gut, and to do it he had to maintain cool and detached from any genuine involvement and pain, even if those implicated and hurt were his own flesh and blood. Since his child was born, he had never helped her with child support. He knew that Alexandra worked, and perhaps he thought that this fact exempted him from any responsibility. Perhaps, this was simply another ruthless and dehumanized manner he had chosen to show them that for him they did not amount to anything.

"I have to go," he said, going to the door.

The sound of the door closing after him made a dry and odd noise. No matter from what angle she looked at him, Alexandra found no excuse to justify his conduct. He was living proof of a penurious and ignoble mind.

THE PROCLAMATION

For all she knew, what happened two months later in October of 1986, was a miracle. Unexpectedly, President Ronald Reagan announced to the nation the enactment of the Amnesty Law allowing illegal aliens to come forth to apply for legal status. It was a day of fiesta and joy. It was as if the providence of God had come to her aid to liberate all of those who, like her, had been anonymous in the country for so long. At last, no more hiding, no more need for lies, no more fear of being discovered, and deported.

Alexandra paced enthusiastically about the room then, gazed at the glaring light of the horizon. How many more like her were "in fiesta" right now, celebrating the vision of a herald of peace-- President Reagan, and the fact that they no longer had to remain in the little cages in which they had confined themselves when they came to the U.S. in order to obtain a better life?

A new hope had begun for the new residents, and also, in a way, a new fling of discrimination. The employers were more cautious and judicious now about hiring foreigners; redoubling their efforts to maintain those that were already hired in craft and entry level jobs, and removing from them any chances for advances.

Among the American people, the new law had augmented their resentment and discord towards the immigrants, whom they still perceived as the same intruders to which the law had granted rights. Perhaps the reason for resentment was that they had mistakenly forgotten that America was still fostering in peoples minds the same hope that carried the first settlers across the ocean- -a view of America as an inextinguishable center of wealth, fortune, opportunity, and prosperity.

105

On the board, Alexandra read about the job opening in Marketing. Just what I was waiting for, she thought, and smiling she went to look for her supervisor. Working as an illegal alien, any job had sufficed. But now, that she had rights as a worker, her options were greater.

Her supervisor was reviewing some papers he had on his desk, when she walked with decisive steps into his office.

"I am sorry to bother you," Alexandra said. "May I come in?"

Her supervisor raised his head, surprised. It wasn't usual to have an employee talk to the supervisor unless it was time for the monthly performance review that the company enforced on each employee to keep track of their working habits and to maintain strict surveillance.

"I just read the memorandum announcing the job opening in the marketing sales department. I want to be considered for that position."

Her supervisor blinked several times, and nervously he deposited on his desk the papers that he had in his hand.

"You can't be assessed," he said, highly overwrought.

"You are not promotable."

"Why not?" Alexandra asked. "I thought all job openings were available for anyone who qualifies for the job. You haven't assessed me; how do you know I'm not promotable?"

"You don't qualify because you have an accent," he answered promptly.

Alexandra blushed as a sudden anger invaded her. "Can you tell me what an accent has to do with intelligence? She snapped, unable to contain herself. "Are you telling me that because I have an accent I have an impediment to function as a normal intelligent human being and that for this reason I am disqualified before being assessed?"

"What I am saying," he said, turning violet, "is that you cannot be assessed for that position because that position is very hard, and with your accent it will be very difficult for you to handle it. Besides, you are very quiet."

"How do you know that the job will be very difficult for me if you don't give me the opportunity to try?" she stated, looking at him as she continued. "And can you tell me what being quiet has to do with intelligence and job performance? As a manager of this company you should have a little more vision and tact than to judge people's intelligence by their accent, their nationality, the way they dress or if they are quiet or not. I thought that in this company all job openings were available for anyone who qualifies regardless of their accent, color or background, but for what you are saying, now I know I was wrong. You have just dispossessed me of any rights to take a test and disqualified me on the grounds that I have an accent, and I think that's illegal." She sighed in exasperation. "Let me tell you one thing," She pointed at him with her index finger. "I am going to fight it. I am going to go to the Union right now to file discrimination charges and then to the Industrial Commission. There is something very wrong here."

"I didn't tell you that," her supervisor said, as nervous as he could get, wiping the sudden coat of sweat that had covered his face. "You are taking it all wrong. Your English is so bad that you are misinterpreting everything I've told you. I don't think that you understand what I am saying at all. You need to take some more English classes to improve your listening, communication, and writing skills."

"I have worked for this company for ten years and I have never had any problem communicating. As far as taking more English classes, we all need to take more English classes. Everyone has room for improvement, don't you agree?"

She walked out of his office, irate. She had the most horrible headache and she was shaky. She was tired and angry about hearing derogatory remarks, and of meeting people like her supervisor. But this time, she was not going to accept this injustice by just folding her arms.

As soon as she got off work, she drove to the Union.

"I came to file a discrimination complaint against Enterprises 2000."

The Union president raised an eyebrow, intrigued, and glanced at her with interest. He was a short man with brilliant blue eyes and black mustache. He moved quickly, he was in his forties and had a rural-like appearance.

"What happened?" He asked with curiosity.

"I applied for a promotion, and my supervisor told me I could not participate in the assessment for the job opening because I have an accent and I am quiet."

The man rubbed his chin nervously. "Write your complaint on these forms, and we'll put them on file." He said as he handed her the forms and a pen. "What kind of position did you apply for?"

"It was a management position in Marketing."

He rubbed his chin again. "If it's a management position, the company can choose anyone they want--we can't do anything about it. The Union doesn't represent management positions, only crafts position jobs."

Alexandra looked at him straight in the eye. "The company can choose anyone they want, perhaps, but I don't think the company has the right to deny me the opportunity to take a test because of my accent. Besides, if they can choose anyone they want for the position, why did they announce it and request anyone interested in it to come forward to be considered?"

"You can file at the Industrial Commission if you want."

"I will," Alexandra answered, standing up. "I wanted to come here first. Thanks for letting me know you can't deal with the problem. I think it is an injustice, and I am going to expose it."

The Union president walked away with obvious discomfort and started to talk to someone else in the office. It was clear that here there was also something fishy. Why have I been paying Union fees for so long, if they can't help me? She wondered.

It didn't matter. She had decided to complain and going to the Industrial Commission the following day was the next step.

106

After Alexandra filed her complaint with the state, things at work changed. The rumors about her complaint had spread around the office. She could tell by the managers' belligerence, and by the co-workers' whispers behind her back as soon as she stepped into the building the next day. From night to morning, "the quiet one," had become for the company a major threat.

Ignoring the looks and whispers, she sat and started her day's work.

"Enterprises 2000, this is Alexandra may I help you?" She had just begun to say, when her supervisor approaching her from behind interrupted the connection.

"Would you come to my office, I need to talk to you." Her supervisor had a rabid fury in his face, and his moves were rapid and rude.

Alexandra stood up surprised and followed him.

"Take a seat." He said ill-tempered pulling a chair for her to sit down. He pulled it with such a force that the chair fell onto the floor. "Gee's!" He exclaimed, lifting it up. "Here," he said, then, sitting behind his desk he began, "due to the seriousness of your complaint against the company, you and I need to maintain this matter in extreme confidentiality. From now on, you can no longer see your personal file for obvious reasons. We have become opponents, and only through attorneys will we be talking about your employee records. Do you understand?"

Alexandra looked at him impassively. He was pale and could hardly contain his hatred. "Yes," Alexandra said.

"You'd better," he warned, "remember that you still work for the company." He stood up looking at her as if she were a pitiful crumb on the floor. "That's all I had. You can go back to your station for now. Remember you can't mention any of this to anybody." He said sternly, walking away.

Alexandra spent the rest of the day in a state of constant unrest. It was a busy day, so busy that there was hardly time to breath between calls. She had the impression as she worked that she was being watched, and that her phone line was being taped and monitored constantly.

107

She needed the job, that's why she kept going, but it wasn't pleasant. She felt the hostility as soon she arrived at work.

"Report to my office when you finish with that call." Her supervisor commanded through the interphone.

She had been working just for a few minutes. She finished the call, and trying to appear calm she stepped into his office.

"Your work is lousy," he said as soon as she sat down, "I have been listening to you this morning, and to tell you the truth, I don't think you are going to make it in this job. You are not following instructions or doing what you are supposed to do. You end the calls without even thanking the customers."

"That's not true!" Alexandra interrupted, appalled by the obvious lie.

"Yes, it is!" He screamed hastily, obviously irritated that she had spoken. "Your calls have been poor every time I have listened to you. This brings your work again to an unsatisfactory level." He glanced at her with disgust. "You can't remain here if you don't improve. You have the weekend to decide what you want to do, if you want to keep on working with the company, or if you want to do something else. This job is very hard, it is not for everyone." He folded his arms as he continued, pushed up his eyeglasses, and rubbed his nose several times. "Do you understand?"

Alexandra looked at him with empty eyes, realizing exactly what he was doing and what the company was after. It was no coincidence that after she filed her complaint with the Industrial Commission, her supervisor had gotten into the habit of calling her two and three times a week to tell her that he had listened to her calls and that her job was second-rate, substandard, and poor.

They are building their case against me, Alexandra thought. This way, when the company presents its case before the court to justify discrimination, they will have well documented that my denial for assessment was due to my ineptitude, not my accent.

"I do understand," she said.

"Fine." He smiled, pleased that his mission had been accomplished. "That is all for now. By the way," he stood up at the time she was stepping out of his office, "here is your first warning for dismissal so you understand the severity of your situation. This is a very strict environment, as I told you. You follow the rules, do what you are told, or you can't be here."

Alexandra took the dismissal and walked to her desk, desolate. The campaign to eliminate her from the picture was not going to stop until she was out. They had chosen to tell her on a daily basis that her capabilities as a functional and working human being had extreme and radical limitations. Giving her bad reports, would give them the excuse they needed to fire her.

"Oppression grows where there is no ground for equality, justice and the exercise of human rights." Alexandra had dared to tell them. "To judge a person's ability by his accent, violates all principles. I have come forward to protest for what I consider an injustice, not only for me, but for all others that have been stopped in their career goals by assigning us a tag of ineptitude due to accents and racial origins."

But to voice this statement had been for them more than outrageous. It had created a well-developed plot already in effect to wipe her out.

108

"Stop working and come into my office." Her supervisor demanded the next morning.

She stopped what she was doing, stood up and followed him in silence. It was eight in the morning. She had been working only for two hours. The meetings in his office had been going on for several months now. She knew what was coming--she was about to receive again a shower of harassing phrases carefully prepared to cause burden and discomfort.

Unlike previous occasions, her supervisor didn't go into his office; he continued walking across the halls, until he reached the end of the building.

"Here," he said despotically pushing open the Union conference door She stepped in silently. He sat at the head of the table where three more men awaited for them, and began, "these are members of the Union, we have been meeting with them for a few weeks to discuss your case. This morning they were asked to listen to you, and we all have agreed in your evaluation. Your work is not satisfactory. Your service level doesn't meet the requirements of this company. You are suspended for three days so it serves you as a time of reflection to understand the severity of your position. Apparently you don't understand,"

"I understand perfectly well," Alexandra exclaimed, loosing her poise. "You want to fire me. If I was really doing such a lousy job as you said, you would give me additional training instead of sending me home. What am I going to do home, learn?" she asked, sarcastically. "Of course, not! Stop the game and the harassment, and fire me now."

"I don't know what you are talking about, but it's irrelevant." He answered rubbing his nose several times. "But as I said, you have until Monday to think about what you are going to do. On Monday when you comeback, we will evaluate your work again.

Remember what I said, you have to improve." He stood up, came towards her a few steps then, handed her a paper. "This is your second warning for dismissal. It's all I have to say. They are here as witnesses. Now, get your things and leave. Don't try to come back before Monday, because the security guard won't let you in."

She took the paper with a trembling hand and went back to her station. No paycheck is big enough to compensate the injury of being constrained, she thought, feeling undermined and humiliated. Freedom is the first priority for every human being, to produce, to create, to live in harmony. The body could be in bondage, but not the soul.

UNEMPLOYMENT

"I quit."

"What?" Sebastian was enraged. "Why did you do something so stupid?"

"I just did," Alexandra said simply. "I couldn't take the harassment anymore. The sole idea of having ten people tapping the phone line to evaluate my calls next Monday, it was more than I could have handled. I didn't want to go through it, even the most apt would have failed under such pre-disposed conditions to find fault, and under such pressure, torture and harassment."

Sebastian looked at her with irritation. "God damn it!" He cursed as he got out of the car, slammed the door with fury, and started to walk away. "You are on your own!"

They had been talking inside her car waiting for Carly to come out from her ballet class when she decided to tell him. His brusque reaction took her so off guard that she didn't have time to respond. She just stared at him in the rearview mirror with vacuous eyes until he was out of sight. He had probably imagined that without having a job, she was going to start asking him for money, and he had taken the best way out for him. A tear gleamed in her eyes.

"I'm glad he is gone," Alexandra said to herself. The last thing she wanted now was to be near the man that even in the most deplorable moments had never been there for her. All she wanted now was to be alone and erase from her mind all harship.

110

"I am sorry, your claim to receive unemployment benefits was denied," the clerk said. "The company you worked for didn't fire you. You quit. That disqualifies you for unemployment benefits."

Alexandra looked at the Job Service clerk in shock. Her head seemed to twirl in helpless desperation. All the hours she spent on the interviews, the forms she filled out to claim for unemployment benefits-- all had been in vain. It was clear at this point that the company where she worked for so many years would continue doing all that was in its capacity to make her life miserable.

She left the Job Service office staggering, still startled by the verdict.

Power is a dangerous tool in the hands of people with racist views and in the hands of the ignorant, she thought as she drove aimlessly. The elephant had finally caught the mouse. The abusive and corrupted practices that Enterprises 2000 administered masqueraded as requirements of the job, the torment they inflicted on her, and the pressure she resigned under for the established system didn't count. She was where Enterprises 2000 wanted her to be, because she had protested for what she had considered a violation of her rights when they had assigned her a tag of ineptitude and deficient racial origin to hinder her from opportunity. It was depressing to witness that despite the fact that slavery was history, there were still some people who made bondage and mistreatment their daily practice. The persecution so magisterially orchestrated and contrived by Enterprises 2000 had succeeded--she was without a job and without money.

111

It bother her to ask for what Sebastian needed to provide, but Sebastian wasn't involved, he came and went as if she were a next door neighbor where he would be just stopping by to say "hi". To have toasted bread, roasted chicken, or warm soup on her table was not of his concern--he ate them daily at the Red Lobster.

"Sebastian, I hate to ask you for some money, but I don't have money to buy groceries."

"Humh, let me check," he said taking out a ten and two five dollar bills from his wallet, "this twenty dollars is the only money I have for my monthly expenses. Giving you the five dollars you need for milk, leaves me with fifteen dollars for the rest of the month," Sebastian said, staring at the bills. He was very pensive and seemed to be confronting the greatest of dilemmas. "Well," he finally said, "I guess I could ask my mother to lend me some money until I get my next pay check at the end of the month. I won't have money for my lunch until she lends me some, but it is okay. Take it," he said handing her the five-dollar bill.

Sebastian hoarded his money. The few occasions when she had asked him for some, he had pinched the pennies out of his pocket with effort, as if they weighed a ton and his hand would be experiencing a twitch of pain to get them out; then, like today, he gave them away hesitantly, always lamenting pitifully, the doleful and precarious state of his finances, and the tremendous deficit that those few dollars he was giving away would cause him.

"Thanks." She said.

112

A brilliant sun announced a new day in Salt Lake City. Carly jumped off her bed, excited.

"Today is the school carnival, mommy," she yelled. "I can't wait."

"I remember," Alexandra said.

"I asked my dad to meet with us there. I hope he doesn't forget."

"He won't forget," Alexandra confirmed. She didn't want to see him, but...

"Mommy, I can't wait. It will be so fun. I'll see you later there."

Alexandra smiled. She would do almost anything to please her daughter. She loved her dearly. She kissed her goodbye, and later that evening as Carly had thought, Alexandra met Sebastian at the school carnival.

"Sebastian," Alexandra said, irritated as soon as she saw him, "you haven't paid for Carly's ballet classes. You still owe Helen one hundred and fourteen dollars from last term plus the new enrollment fee. We need to pay her."

Sebastian raised his hands to rub his forehead as he closed his eyes. Alexandra knew this gesture well, and knew he was trying to avoid the issue.

"I don't have any money," he answered. "The only thing I can do is borrow fifty dollars from my son Kris and pay her that."

Alexandra did not turn to see him. She looked in front, trying to contain her anger and humiliation.

"Every week I give my mother my check and she hands me one hundred dollars for any expenses I may have during the month," he said.

She stared at him intently. How many times since she had been unemployed had she heard him saying the same thing? It had been a year, to be exact, since he started to pay eighty-four dollars every three months for Carly's ballet class.

"That leaves me twenty-five dollars for expenses each week," he continued as his eyes wandered over the school landscape. "We have to face it--we are very short of money. We can no longer spend the fourteen dollars to have dinner out on Saturday, and save that money for Helen."

Alexandra avoided looking at him to hide the pain she was feeling.

"I have been using my credit cards, even when I promised my mother I wasn't going to use them. I don't know how I am going to face her." Sebastian concluded.

Alexandra abruptly broke into laughter. "What I want to know is," she said with sarcasm, " when, once and for all, are you going to ask your mother to stop interfering in your life? You're not a baby anymore. You don't need your mother to control your money, or to tell you what to say, what to do, whom to love. You are old enough to make those determinations. Let me tell you one more thing. It irritates me to hear you say that you are so poor that you always have to borrow from your sons to meet your daily expenses, because nobody believes that."

Sebastian blushed. His hands kept rubbing his forehead. His eyes were closed.

"Your sons don't make more money than you do. You make pretty good money--what do you do with it?" she screamed. "I don't see you wearing expensive clothes or buying new cars."

"I have to pay my credit cards," he said briefly, as though talking to himself.

"Sebastian," Alexandra said, looking at him impatiently, "you can pay all your credit cards with one month of your salary, and please don't tell me otherwise. This is ridiculous! It would be much better if you'd just tell me that you don't want us, and that it hurts you to spend money on us."

Sebastian now looked tense and defensive. His eyes had a blur that fell over them when bothersome thoughts crossed his mind. It didn't matter; Alexandra was tired of keeping quiet and of accepting the lies and excuses that she could not believe.

"I know what you are thinking," she said with pain as she walked, looking around for Carly, who had left them to run after her friends as soon as they met at the school ground. "Your mother is right when she tells you, 'Alexandra just wants your money. Don't give her anything, or pretty soon she will want your house.' Am I not right, Sebastian? Doesn't she tell you that?"

Sebastian walked behind Alexandra silently, with a submissive attitude.

There were a lot of people, laughter, music, food, and games. People she knew here and there said hello, glancing at Sebastian with curiosity.

"I don't know about you," Alexandra said with more sorrow than anger, "but it feels weird not to be able to introduce you to people as my husband. That is your choice and your fault, not mine. If I had a job, I wouldn't ask you for money. I've never asked you for anything when I had a job. You started to pay for Carly's classes a year ago when I lost my job, and that amounts to 28 dollars a month--not a whole lot to give to your daughter."

She couldn't stop. His wretchedness this time was too much.

"I am not sure about you," Alexandra continued with sarcasm, "but it is very embarrassing that people think you are so poor that you don't have 28 dollars a month to spend on your daughter."

She turned to look at him suddenly; Sebastian was pale, but he remained silent.

"Don't worry," Alexandra patted his back, trying to hide her tears. "I'll see what I can do. You don't have to go broke for our expenses. I will get the money to pay Helen, the new enrollment fee, and what you owed her six moths ago."

She walked faster, calling and looking for her daughter in the crowd. She left Sebastian behind; all of a sudden she wanted to run and hide.

"Carly," Alexandra said with relief, finding her daughter, "I want to go home. It is getting late and it's cold."

"Just a little longer, mommy, just a little longer," her daughter pleaded.

"O.k." Alexandra said. There was no point in ruining her daughter's fun. "I am going to the car to get my sweater; I will wait for you there."

She turned and stepped into Sebastian, who stood smiling lovingly at Carly.

"I'll stay with you, darling," he said to his daughter.

Carly nodded and ran back to meet her friends. Alexandra did not look at Sebastian. She passed him and walked away.

In the distance, the horizon was gold, like an immense lake of fire. She wiped away her tears angrily. She didn't want to think, but her heart was burning with pain. Her behavior was absurd. Time and again Sebastian had showed her that he didn't love them, but when she was with him, she always succumbed to her passion. At Sebastian's side, she had learned how destructive and demeaning loving could sometimes be.

Alexandra looked at the horizon. The golden clouds were now dimmer and the sun had almost disappeared beneath the Great Salt Lake devoured under silvery shadows. Why was Carly taking so long? She shook her head trying to erase the cruel recollections.

"Mommy! Mommy! I had the greatest time!" Carly screamed as she opened the car door, getting in. "Thanks for waiting. I hope they have another carnival next week, but I know they won't. I have to wait until the next year. That's awful!"

"Well," Alexandra said, smiling, "something else will come up, you'll see."

She started the engine and drove home.

113

Going in search of a job in the 90's was not the same as getting a job in the 80's. In the 90's, looking for a job was almost like preparing for a battle. Degrees and training were not enough.

For one thing, the economic situation had changed drastically. Computers were taking over in the marketplace displacing labor forces. And secondly, there was a bitter spurt of all sorts of societal stereotypes, possibly stimulated by The Amnesty Law and by the sudden flare-up of a myriad of separatist groups that emphasized differences and demanded special rights.

Perhaps the major tragedy of life is precisely that. Alexandra reflected as she drove looking for a job. That hardly anyone feels part of the immense human race, and that almost everyone lets their social groups, church groups, race groups, money groups, handicap groups, political groups, and gender groups isolate them from one another.

The search for a job for her had been tedious and tiresome. Everywhere she had gone to apply, they all had said "we'll give you a call," but no one had called.

Getting a job nowadays was harder than it ever was, she concluded in desperation as the days turned into weeks and the weeks to months without having been called to a single job interview. Something must be wrong, but what? She pondered, as she went from place to place. "That's it!" She exclaimed, remembering what they told her at Enterprises 2000 the day she went to resign. "It's better for your record if you resign than to be fired." She did not understand what they meant then, but now she did, seeing the light for the first time in months. Enterprises 2000 had been giving bad referrals about her.

Without noticing, she drove under the freeway. The homeless had established a small community there. She stared at them; they were gathered in small groups of four and five, perhaps to share with others like themselves their desolation and misfortune. Looking at them, it wasn't difficult for Alexandra to recall her father. He had been on the street like them, despoiled and castrated of chance by labels and tragedy. For a spectator, it was easy to criticize and be scandalized by their deplorable look, but no one really knew how hard it was to be on the street, stigmatized by society and fighting against labels and false perceptions, with hungry stomachs and woeful souls.

"My unemployment is so clear, now." She said to herself. "I demanded fair treatment, and a year later, they are still punishing me for my audacity." Right there and then, she made the decision to delete Enterprises 2000 from her job applications.

114

"Tell us about yourself." One of the interviewers said.

Alexandra had seen the clinic job opening in "The Tribune" and she had gone to file an application.

The eyes of the interviewers were focused on her attentively and she forced herself to appear calm and natural. It had been so ironic, and depressing looking for a job, almost hilarious—too many requirements and questions for a wage of 4.25 an hour. Alexandra breathed deeply and uttered easily what she had decided to say.

"I don't have any work experience," Alexandra said, looking directly into their eyes. "I have been married for ten years; I am now divorced and ready to come back into the work force."

The ten years she had devoted to working for Enterprises 2000 with those words, had been erased. All she wanted was a better job opportunity with them, but the sole act of demanding it, had shattered her world and robbed her of the resources she needed to be happy. "To work in an environment of equality is so important," she told them before she quit, "where employees feel capable of doing a good job without the constant oppression of having someone telling them how deficiently they do things and how inadequate and inept they are.." The voice of the interviewers brought her back to reality.

"The pay is not high but you'll have medical insurance." One explained.

Something is better than nothing, She thought, as she shook their hand to thank them. At least I will have a few dollars to pay the most essential bills. The lie had paid off--they hired her to work in the clinic.

The immoderate laughs of Marsha and Shirley stopped her recollections. They were talking loudly, telling each other bluntly about their sexual lives with their husbands. Alexandra felt sick.

Listening to them everyday was almost like having a rope around her neck. It was hard to take it. This job was certainly not all that she expected of life.

WORK TALES

Alexandra woke up early in the morning, took her little daughter to school, and, as she did every day, drove to the clinic. She lived on the east side of Salt Lake City so it only took her a few minutes to get there. It was dreadful to walk in and feel the asperity that was reflected in the unfriendly faces of Shirley and Marsha.

"Hello," Alexandra greeted as she passed them, but Marsha and Shirley continued to chat, pretending not to see her.

Another day, Alexandra thought, feeling the heavy weight of the hours ahead. She pulled the list of the patient appointments for the day and began to work silently. Shirley was sitting with her legs resting on the front desk counter, complaining about her pregnancy ills and eating as usual. She was fat, short, very talkative, and fond of gossiping. She had a big head and thick, reddish, disheveled hair that fell over her shoulders, giving her a lion-like appearance. Her nose was always sweaty and red, and when she moved, she panted constantly as though she were in a rush, clamoring to all about her good-natured husband, her sex life, and her mother-in-law's infamous treatment towards her.

Fed up with such distasteful remarks, Alexandra made up her mind to go to the clinic's personnel department to request a transfer to any of the available job openings. The clinic's executive director was a church acquaintance; they weren't friends, but they said hello occasionally.

"It is not what you know, but who you know," Alexandra heard many times while working for Enterprises 2000. And this, she thought, is a good opportunity to verify it.

Contrary to her expectations, Carol treated her as if she hadn't seen her before. Behind the desk, and protected by her executive title, the clinic's executive director was disinterested and formal.

"You have to direct your request for transfer to Anna in Personnel," Carol said, moving her hands with the attitude of those who, after given a little power, feel superior to others. She was about fifty years old. She had blond curly hair, and at first sight was fair and pleasant in appearance. "It is up to her to make the final decision for the new candidate. I can't do anything. I am sorry." With this, she stood up as though there was nothing else to be discussed, opened the upper desk drawer of her desk, took some papers out, and looked at her watch as if in a hurry.

Alexandra thanked her politely and walked out of the office smiling, hiding her disappointment. The truth was that she felt like crying.

In Personnel, Anna also turned down her application.

"No one has been selected for the position that you want yet," said Anna formally, "but we are expecting to find within the applicants someone with more expertise than you."

Alexandra closed her eyes momentarily, feeling very tired. Life as a single parent, and life in general, was unfair and difficult. Going to school was a relief to the tension and the dissatisfaction she usually felt. Learning was a short rest to her thoughts, and the door she needed to explore new horizons. It was a pleasure to read, to hear the teachers lecture, and to close her eyes and imagine the realization of her dreams in laughter, success, and wonder.

Outside the clinic's corporate office, the green of the trees was vibrant. Spring was once more here, and for Alexandra there was nothing more beautiful than the vision of a bird suspended in the vast sky, the mountains in the twilight, or her children.

116

At the clinic, tensions increased. There was no teamwork or job ethics to provide good service or to create good employee relationships. The nurses backstabbed the doctors, the doctors did the same to the nurses, and Marsha and Shirley at the front desk backstabbed everyone who came in contact with them.

"Only Marsha and I have the key to the safe," Shirley told Alexandra, emphasizing each word. "The last time we gave the combination to the other Mexican who worked here before you, money was always missing."

Alexandra bit her tongue, determined not to respond, but felt her blood boiling. Only because of need did she keep on going to work, but it was very difficult to understand how people without any training or finesse could be in charge.

"I am sorry," Marsha and Shirley would invariably say to the poorest and most needy, "the doctors are very busy today. There is no way they can get to see you today without an appointment. The next available appointment won't be for a month."

It was hard to listen without being able to say anything, disguising awareness with indifference. What they said to people were lies, but Marsha and Shirley seemed to enjoy seeing destitute people suffering, and the helpless look reflected in their astonished eyes when they were turned down. In no other place had Alexandra realized as strongly as in this clinic that the system worked only for the powerful and the rich, with only the crumbs left for the needy. The poor had no breaks; they were forced to remain cut off from opportunity. As for Alexandra, since she was Mexican, Marsha and Shirley had always treated her as a second-class human being with limited intelligence to understand how to file, how to match colors, or how to put pencils in the right place.

It was tiring to put up with their remarks and keep quiet. Whenever she turned her back, Marsha and Shirley managed to mess with her work. Then they accused her, pointing out how incapable she was.

"Mommy, I am sorry you have to go through all of this at work." Carly said, kissing her with loving concern and sadness when Alexandra related to her what those women said and did in the clinic. Carly was now eleven years old, sensitive and beautiful.

Her smile and love always kept Alexandra going. Regardless of background or color of skin, Alexandra had taught her children that everyone--the homeless, the drug addicts, or the homosexuals--deserved to be treated with respect and human dignity. She was glad that Franco was on his mission for the church, so he didn't have to pass through all of this. It was just not pleasant.

117

When she arrived at work the next morning, Alexandra noticed the unusual whispering and the contemptuous looks that Marsha and Shirley gave her. She wasn't integrated as part of the group, and didn't participate in their superficial talks or in their backbiting sessions. She had kept apart, doing her work in silence, ignoring their constant put downs and criticisms.

"They want you at administration at 10:00 o'clock," Shirley mumbled in Alexandra's ear mysteriously.

Shirley had the attitude of those who, having perpetrated evil, enjoy every minute of their deed without conscience. Alexandra briefly looked at her and said nothing.

She had surmised their conspiracy by the hatred she felt from them and the things Marsha had told her just a few days ago.

"We don't want you here," Marsha had finally confessed hysterically, when Alexandra, no longer able to accept their lies interrupted Marsha's customary denial to provide service to a homeless.

"One moment, sir," Alexandra had said with compassion. "Don't leave. Let me talk to the doctor; I am sure he will manage to see you today. Disease doesn't set appointments."

The eyes of the man in rags lit up with gratefulness.

"Thank you, Miss." He said humbly.

Marsha looked at Alexandra, livid with hatred. Her mouth had twitched in rage and disbelief.

"You can't do that!" Marsha yelled, trembling and breathing heavily, as though she were all of a sudden having an attack. "It's against the rules! Where are you going? Come back!"

Alexandra, walking down the hall, abruptly stopped and slowly returned to the front desk, where Marsha stood shaking violently.

"Shut up!" Alexandra said.

For a fraction of a second, Marsha looked astonished.

"We don't want you here!" she exploded again, stomping on the floor. "You are not like us, we want an American!"

But Alexandra, ignoring the frantic and ridiculous screams, disappeared down the hall to call a doctor.

It doesn't matter if they fire me, Alexandra reflected as she continued to file the lab work in silence. She collected the last morning appointment charts and set them carefully on the desk. Injustice had always awakened in her strong feelings of disgust and rebellion, and also a sharp pain, as though a knife was cutting her inside. It was sad, Alexandra realized, but this was the daily bread of the poor, receiving put-downs in response to their disgraceful condition as though disgrace was only the result of their choices and not the result of social victimization that prevented them from getting ahead.

She went to the locker room and grabbed her purse. It was thirty minutes past nine, just enough time to make it to the administration building. She closed the clinic's door quietly and got into her car. The administration building was on the west part of town. From the downtown clinic, driving on the freeway, it took around fifteen minutes to get there. She hadn't been in that building since she was hired.

When Alexandra arrived, Shirley and Anna were standing at the end of the main corridor. They were whispering, and when they saw her, their murmuring stopped. It was clear that they had been waiting impatiently for her arrival. Alexandra walked towards them without hurry and greeted them politely.

"Let's go in this room to get started," Anna said. They walked into a room that was situated at the right side of the hallway and took seats behind the oval table.

"We just want to tell you," Anna began, "that we have decided to terminate you."

Alexandra looked at them, undaunted.

"I have been informed by Shirley," Anna continued, trying to be professional, "that your performance at the clinic is not what we had expected." She paused and shuffled some papers. "There are a lot of complaints about you." Ana seemed nervous and a little irate, and as she spoke, she glanced from time to time at Shirley as though to elicit her reaction.

Anna was in charge of hiring. Since the first time Alexandra met her, Ana had always worn the same dress. It was black, long and had a silky-transparent appearance. Her shoes were black, pointed, with golden heels. She had her hair dyed in brilliant orange, cut too close to her scalp. She was about 4 feet 4 inches tall, had a little head, and big, almost gigantic ears from which she hung immense circular earnings.

"You need to sign here and here, where you agree to your dismissal for not measuring up to work standards." Anna continued with fake formality. She handed Alexandra the piece of paper with impatience.

Alexandra took the paper calmly, studied it for a second, looked at Shirley intently then, set it on the table.

"I won't sign it," Alexandra said, erasing the half smile of triumph on Shirley's face. "I don't agree with what it says."

"Well, whatever," replied Anna sharply. She appeared tremendously irritated. "We wish you luck." She rose to her feet, pale with ire, and stormed towards the door, abruptly followed by Shirley.

"Thanks," Alexandra answered, standing up and depositing her locker key on the table. As soon as she released the key, her mood brightened. "Good day," she said courteously as she passed Anna and Shirley then she smiled gracefully as she walked out.

On her way home, Alexandra pulled into a fast food restaurant and ordered a sandwich and a soft drink. She gave a few bites to her sandwich, drank her drink and went back to her car. Driving from the west part of the city, the mountains in the east rose like a powerful and protective curtain in front of her. It was good to look at their tops and distract her mind, imagining how and when they were formed, and how and when life evolved on earth.

When she got home, she kissed and hugged her daughter. Still holding Carly. Alexandra took a deep breath. The future was in front of her again, bringing to her door a new challenge.

118

As they were eating Alexandra saw Sebastian. He was getting out of his car.

"There's dad!" Carly screamed as she ran to hide behind the entrance door to scare her dad.

Alexandra cleaned the table rapidly then walked back into the dinning room.

Sebastian by that time opened the door.

"Boooohhh!" Carly screamed.

Sebastian was smiling.

Carly laughed. "I got you, didn't I? You jerked. You looked so funny."

"Hi," Alexandra said putting back the vase of flowers on the center of the table.

"Hi," he answered as he went to the living room to sit near his daughter.

"I was fired today." Alexandra said following them into the living room, "I saw it coming, remember I told you? It was the works of those two intriguing characters that didn't want me there. I should be upset Sebastian, but I'm not. This gives me change to look for a better job, don't you think so?"

Sebastian remained silent for a few seconds looking at the floor. He had such a grave expression on his face that, for a moment Alexandra thought that what she said had dawned on him for the first time. "What are you thinking Sebastian?" She asked hopefully.

"I'm thinking," Sebastian said marking each word, and deeply concern with his procrastination, "that my kitchen needs some cleaning. I haven't cleaned it for so long, and it's really dirty."

His response was by no means a surprise, but it offended her. "Yes," she nodded biting her lips and the pain that his disregard caused her, "It's kind of dirty; you need to clean it."

"Yeah," he exclaimed. "Here I go."

He had stood up and reached for the door with quick steps followed by Carly.

"Dad," Carly said breaking into tears. "We won't have money to pay the rent and to buy food until my mother gets another job. I'm scared, I don't know what we are going to do."

"Yes, I know." he said scratching his hair with indifference before he went out without recoil, "Life is hard."

119

Life was hard, but it was getting better by the minute. She was here celebrating this unique moment with her children. Alexandra smiled confidently and looked up. Carly and Franco were sitting on the second floor of the Assembly Hall smiling at her with pride. Just in time for her graduation, a few days ago, Franco came back from his mission. She wiped her tears of joy trying to contain the mad throbbing of her heart. In front of her the College choir was singing praises to God. The commencement ceremony had begun.

"Alexandra Marquez." The announcer called.

Alexandra stood up and walked to the pulpit to receive from the hands of the Dean, her Bachelor's Diploma. Holding it on high she waved at Carly and Franco and smiled. It was a moment of glory and the end of a journey that had began when she decided to take the first night class. Crying, at the end of the ceremony, she went running to hold her children. She would have wanted to plaster her very soul in the hugs she gave them. She simply adored them. Holding hands with them, they came out from the Assembly Hall and walked around the Temple Square. She looked up; the sky had, as always, that magical touch of infinite, of beyond, of peace, of wonder and hope. It was so blue--with thin patches of clouds as light strokes of white over a canvas and, the Temple, against the silhouette of light, stood grandiose and heavenly. Life was simply grand.

THE TRIAL

All dressed up, there she was at nine o'clock at her attorney's office as she was required shaking hands with them.

"Ready?" one of the attorneys asked looking at her.

"Ready," Alexandra said half smiling.

"All right, let's go."

They walked across the street to the Federal Courthouse. She was not nervous. It was the day of the trial and she was ready to testify. She had been waiting for this moment since she filed her complaint with the State in 1991--four years to be exact. Passing the security guards inspection at the Courthouse they went into the courtroom. Over the judge's seat, attached to the wall, her eyes rested upon the impressive seal of justice. It was magnanimous, and certainly an inspiring token of law, order, and rule. Alexandra took her seat silently and looked around. She, and the two court typists were the only women in the room. Across the room, right in front of her, sat three Union leaders, two of the perpetrator managers, and the five defense attorneys. She took a pen and played with it. Her two attorneys and the five attorneys representing Enterprises 2000 had met in the middle of the courtroom to talk forming like a small circle. They all had their hands in their pockets, stood with their legs spread apart, and swayed their bodies as they talked with noted importance. The head company attorney sent her a look that could have pulverized her. After all, she was like a microbe he wanted to exterminate, to prove his mastery of law as a defense attorney. Alexandra sustained his look impassively. It was so easy to sense his arrogance. He stood up with his head at an inclination of thirty-five degrees above the heads of the rest. At this point, all the attorneys seemingly agreed upon something because they broke the circle, and went to take their posts behind their desks as they opened suitcases and books, buttoned and unbuttoned their jackets, and put their ties in place in some kind of rush expectancy.

Her attorneys weren't talking much to her. They sat at her side in silence, and she wondered about their demeanor. At first, they were very interested in her case. Then, they changed. They seemed reluctant and withdrawn, as if they wanted to persuade her to let things go or to bend her stand. It happened a few months before the trial.

"Enterprises 2000 are proposing you a settlement," one of her attorneys said, acting as the speaker, one day she met with them, "we think you should take it. If you do, you don't have to go to trial."

The statement bothered her. She had come to their office to discuss the preliminaries, not a settlement. She looked at him incredulously.

"If you are asking me is to give in, my answer is no! I won't give in."

"Well, think about it," her attorney insisted, "you don't know if you are going to win. If you go to trial you might not win and you will loose what they are offering you now."

Alexandra blushed. She felt insulted and crushed. There was no money in the world enough to buy her.

"Whether I win or loose, I want to go to trial. It's not the money I am after, it is the principle—I'm a true supporter of The Constitution."

"Again," her attorney said overlooking her statement, "it's a good offer and we know you need money. All you need to do is to sign this document. No trial, no questions. What do you say? If you don't accept this now, they might change their minds and you will loose."

Alexandra smiled. "Imagine where we would be if the founding fathers would have given up or sold their post to the best bidder--we wouldn't be here enjoying civil liberties now." She wasn't susceptible to bribes, moreover, when they were to sustain dishonesty and faulty notions of justice.

The attorneys looked at each other perplexed, then at her.

"Do you just want to role the dice?" the speaker asked.

"Yes," she said. "I want to role the dice."
"Win or loose?"
"Win or loose." She said.
"Are you sure?"
"I'm sure."

She left their office hurt and confused. What side were they on? Regardless of the outcome she had decided to testify. The ideas of honor and a noble cause excited her. It sent goose pumps through her spine. She was perhaps as passionate as Patrick Henry who said, "Give me liberty or give me death." She didn't know about her attorneys.

As she began to testify of the injustice during trial, almost immediately, the attorneys requested a conference with the judge. Upon their return, Alexandra's attorneys said:

"You are not going to testify."

"Why not?"

"You entered the country as an illegal alien--you don't have a change to win. We are going to accept a settlement."

Alexandra looked at them perplexed, "I don't want a settlement; I want to testify and make a stand."

"You can't."

She looked at them intently waiting for an explanation.

"Why not?" she asked.

"It's a matter of power, not a matter of principle." One of them said. He wasn't looking at her when he said it.

After spending half a day in court discussing what seemed to her pre-arranged agreements, they left the Court House behind, and what had been, until a few hours ago, her fight to sustain the principles for which The Constitution stands. What happened there, still made no sense to her, but now it was a thing of the past.

The terms and conditions of the settlement that wiped out her insurrection were sealed to prevent perhaps bad publicity for the company.

FREE AT LAST

With flowers in her hand Alexandra stepped into the Cemetery. She walked a few steps through the path in the middle and stopped near the fresh grave. It was Sebastian's. It was after one of their altercations about money, a few months back, that he stopped his visits. Watching the local news she heard about his death. He and the woman that was with him had died in the awful car crash. She left the flowers in the vase and walked away. She had touched heaven and hell in his arms. Now, nothing remained-- his remembrance was like a dream within a dream. She was free. Free at last and strong. She walked with quick and firm steps towards the gate. Carly and Franco were waiting for her there. They were her real true loves. What wealth in the whole world could be greater than them?

"None," she said to herself.

About the Author

Irma Noriega grew up in Mexico City. She has lived in the United States for the last twenty-two years. She has a BA in Communications from the Westminster College and an AS in Marketing Management from the L.D.S. Business College. Noriega teaches ESL to foreign students and lives in Salt Lake with her son and daughter.